A TANGLED WEB

Books by Jane Peart

The Brides of Montclair Series
Valiant Bride
Ransomed Bride
Fortune's Bride
Folly's Bride
Yankee Bride/Rebel Bride
Gallant Bride
Shadow Bride
Destiny's Bride
Jubilee Bride
Mirror Bride
Hero's Bride
Senator's Bride
Daring Bride
Courageous Bride
A Montclair Homecoming

The Westward Dreams Series
Runaway Heart
Promise of the Valley
Where Tomorrow Waits
A Distant Dawn
Undaunted Spirit

The American Quilt Series
The Pattern
The Pledge
The Promise

A TANGLED WEB

JANE PEART

GRAND RAPIDS, MICHIGAN 49530

ZONDERVAN

A Tangled Web
Copyright © 2001 by Jane Peart

Requests for information should be addressed to:

Zondervan, *Grand Rapids, Michigan 49530*

Library of Congress Cataloging-in-Publication Data
Peart, Jane.
    A tangled web / Jane Peart.
       p. cm.
    ISBN 0-310-22013-0
    1. Women pioneers—Fiction. 2. Restaurants—Fiction. 3. Waitresses—Fiction.
I. Title.
PS3566.E238 T3 2001
813'.54—dc21   2001017682

Interior design by Todd Sprague

Printed in the United States of America

01 02 03 04 05 06 /❖ DC/ 10 9 8 7 6 5 4 3 2

ACKNOWLEDGMENTS

It is with deep gratitude the author acknowledges the following books, which proved invaluable in filling in the background of this story: *A Great and Shining Road: The Epic Story of the Transcontinental Railroad* by John Hoyt Williams; *West by Rail* by William Fraser Rae; *Inventing the Southwest: The Fred Harvey Company and Native American Art* by Kathleen L. Howard and Diana F. Pardue; and *The Harvey Girls: Women Who Opened the West* by Lesley Poling-Kempes.

A special thanks also to Paul Philippi, computer consultant, who rescued this manuscript when my hard drive crashed.

PREFACE

When the first transcontinental railroad was completed in 1869, it transformed life in the United States. We became a mobile society. Americans were able to travel from one coast to the other—however, not always with comfort and enjoyment.

By opening a chain of restaurants and hotels along the Santa Fe Railroad, Fred Harvey filled that need. He provided train passengers with first-class dining facilities and delicious food elegantly served by an elite class of waitresses called the Harvey Girls.

I have set my novel in the early part of the twentieth century, when the Harvey House chain was well established throughout the Southwest, and its staff of young women highly regarded. I have taken the liberty of using basic facts and fictionalizing them, moving locations and events to make an interesting story I hope you will enjoy.

PART
ONE

ONE

SEPTEMBER 1903

The huge Chicago railroad station teemed with passengers hurrying to catch their trains. Darcy Welburne, a slim, pretty young woman, stood on the platform, anxiously studying the departure schedule. Clutched tightly in her hand was her ticket for the Santa Fe Railway line taking her to her destination: Juniper Junction, Kansas. Her heart was thundering. Just turned twenty, she had never before traveled alone nor more than thirty miles from her home in eastern Tennessee. Had she made a terrible mistake? Well, it was too late to wonder, too late to change her mind. She was on her way now. However, she had no idea that this journey would alter her life forever.

"Boarding now for Atchison, Topeka, Santa Fe, and all points between," the conductor announced. As Darcy showed him her ticket, he commented, "Juniper Junction, eh? That's just a ten-minute whistle-stop, little lady." Somehow that didn't make her feel any better.

She mounted the steps to her coach. Juggling her suitcase and valise, she made her way down the aisle, looking for a vacant seat.

At the end of the car she found an empty one. She set down her smaller bag, then lifted the larger one into the overhead rack. A little out of breath from the effort, she started to sit down, when she saw a tract lying on her seat.

Printed in large bold letters on the front were the words "You need Jesus." *Probably left there by some zealot,* she thought. She picked it up and distractedly put it in her handbag with her ticket stub. Then she sat down and leaned her head back on the worn, green upholstered seat.

With a jolting lurch the train started forward, moving through the railroad yard. Outside the city it began to pick up speed, taking Darcy hundreds of miles from home and the man she loved. She fought the beginnings of homesickness. After all, this was her own decision. Nobody had forced her to go. In fact, most of the people she knew had practically begged her not to leave Willowdale.

Darcy stared out the sooty window. With the clickety-clack of the train's wheels, she could hear her mother's voice endlessly repeating, "Mark my words—you'll regret it."

It had been an impulsive decision to break her engagement to Grady Thomas, to apply for a teaching position in

Kansas. But a promise was a promise, and Grady had broken his promise to her not to run for sheriff.

How could he have done this to her? He knew how she felt about politics after having lived with her uncle the judge, who had to run for reelection every four years.

Their terrible quarrel rushed back to her. She had never been so angry. Certainly it was a righteous anger.

"You gave me your *word!*" she accused.

"I know I did, but—"

"There are no buts to a promise."

"Ah, Darcy, come on—a man's got to think of his future, don't he? Try to better himself? If I make sheriff, it will be for you too! Our future."

"Being in politics is *not* my future! I had enough of it from the time I was a little girl and Mama and I moved in with Aunt Maude and Uncle Henry. I saw firsthand what kind of life politics is for the wife, and I knew I didn't want what Aunt Maude put up with. Riffraff of all kinds parading in and out of the house any time of night or day. Fixing meals for ten or twenty or more at the drop of a hat. Having him gone to rallies, electioneering barbecues, and picnics all up and down the county six months out of every year. Having people banging on the front door at midnight, getting threatening letters besides. And being a sheriff's wife would probably be even worse. No, thank you. I'm not marrying a politician. So you can forget marriage and forget engagement." Out of breath, she had tugged off the garnet solitaire from the third finger of her left hand and held it out to Grady. "Here's your ring back!"

"Ah, honey, you don't mean that—"

"I never meant anything so much in my life!" she had flung back at him.

Grady should have known better. After all, they had known each other since childhood. He should have known Darcy wouldn't take his broken promise lightly.

Everyone was stunned at what she did, and further shocked when she got the acceptance letter from the Juniper Junction school board.

Her mother was not the only person who had argued against the broken engagement, her decision to leave Willowdale. Her spinster aunt Sadie had confided sadly, "You'll be sorry. I speak from my own experience. I did the same thing at eighteen and look at me now—a dried-up old maid living with relatives, with no home to call my own, no man to provide for me, no children to cuddle . . ."

Her Uncle Henry was outraged. "Don't a man have the right to make his own choice of how he makes a living? It's not a woman's place to tell him. Besides, sheriffs get paid a good salary, have standing in the community—a young woman could do a lot worse. A whole lot worse."

Even her best friend Carly Hampton, who had always admired Darcy's gumption, was taken aback. "I can't believe you're letting go a man that almost every girl in town has set her cap for one time or another. Somebody else's bound to snap him up quick as you can say fiddle!"

"Let them, then!" Darcy had retorted with a toss of her head. "Who'd want a man who can't keep a promise?"

She'd been mighty sure of herself when she'd said those words, sure that Grady would withdraw from the sheriff's race. But then, Grady could be stubborn too. He'd let her go, hadn't he? Now she wondered if maybe she'd spoken too hastily, burned her bridges too recklessly.

A picture of her former fiancé flashed into her mind. At six foot two Grady carried his height with a lanky ease. He was handsome in a rugged, outdoorsy way. His features were regular and his blue eyes most always held merriment. He was capable of boyish pranks as well as a genuine sweetness. In spite of herself, Darcy's heart softened a little as she remembered his bewildered expression at her ultimatum. But it was his own fault. Maybe this would teach him a lesson.

Deaf to entreaties from family and friends, she had packed, bought her ticket, and was on her way. A *long* way from Willowdale, her hometown, where she had been born, grown up, gone to school, fallen in love.

As the train rattled through the unfamiliar countryside, Darcy's troubled thoughts turned to the place that had been home to her since she was five years old.

The big, square, white frame house, built in 1850 by Joshia Baldwin, stood a block from Main Street. It was referred to by the townsfolk as the Beehive, not only because of the dome-shaped cupola on its roof but also because three generations of the Baldwins had occupied it. The matriarch Beatrice, a formidable old lady of seventy known as Grandma Bee, still lived there. Her three daughters made their home there, too: Maude, the oldest, married to Judge Henry Roscoe, who as a young lawyer and a new bridegroom had moved into his mother-in-law's house; Sadie, who had never married; and Ellen, who when widowed had returned home with her little girl. The household at 220 Elm Street was a close-knit one. That is why Darcy's decision had caused such an upset.

She had grown up surrounded by love and caring. Although she had sometimes found it cloying and almost smothering, still she knew she would miss it all. But there was no time for second thoughts now. As Grandma Bee was fond of saying, "No use crying over spilled milk." She was on her way. She had to think it was the right choice, that she hadn't made a dreadful mistake.

The hours on the train were tedious and long. Darcy found herself nodding off once or twice. Suddenly she was alerted by the conductor's voice loudly calling out, "Juniper Junction!" The train was slowing to a stop. This was it. She had reached her destination.

TWO

Darcy quickly gathered her belongings and hurried to the coach door and stepped down from the train onto the platform. A violent gust of wind whipped her skirt and blew sand into her face. She dropped her valise to grab the brim of her small feathered hat to keep it from flying off her head.

Within minutes the train started up again and moved down the track, disappearing around the bend, leaving her standing forlornly on the deserted platform. Her trunk, evidently tossed off the baggage car, stood at the end of the platform. There were no porters, no other passengers. In fact, there was no one in sight. Was she the only person getting off here?

Propelled by the strong wind at her back and wobbling slightly in her high-heeled boots on the uneven boards, she teetered toward the yellow frame station house.

It took all her strength to wrest open the door, pushing against it with her shoulder. Inside it was empty except for the man behind the ticket window. She walked over to the counter and said politely, "Excuse me, sir. I'd like some information."

At first there was no indication that he had heard her. Then slowly he shifted the green eyeshade he wore and looked up at her. "What's that?"

"Is there somewhere I could get a room, freshen up?"

He frowned as if puzzled. "Freshen up, eh? You fixin' on stayin' long?"

"Well, that depends."

"Depends?" He peered at her through wire-rimmed glasses.

"Actually, it depends on whether—" Darcy halted. Why go into all this with the railroad station clerk? "You see, I've been on the train a long time, and—" Again she stopped. Of course he knew that. "I'd just like a room to— the reason doesn't matter. Could you simply tell me if there is a place nearby where I could rent a room?"

He squinted and gave her a calculating look.

Darcy felt as though he were making an inventory of her with her fashionable gray traveling suit and smart little hat. Not your everyday sight in a town like this, she supposed.

He jerked his thumb over his shoulder.

"The Grand's the only hotel in town. Jest acrost the street. I guess that'll do you."

"Thank you," she said coolly, wondering if all residents of this town were as unhelpful to strangers. However, she needed some more information, and he was the only one around at the moment.

"By the way, could you please tell me when the school board meets?"

"Humph, the school board?" He paused a second before answering. "Tonight at the town hall. Six-thirty sharp." Curiosity glinted in his narrowed eyes. He seemed about to ask her why she wanted to know, but Darcy turned away to avoid answering. Why should she explain to this person who had treated her in such an unfriendly manner? Then, remembering one of Grandma Bee's favorite sayings, "You can catch more flies with honey than with vinegar," Darcy returned to the ticket counter. It was always important to make a good impression. Who knew but that this man might be a member of the school board? In small communities the most unlikely people sometimes held positions of influence. Smiling her sweetest, Darcy said, "I'm here to fill the position for the grammar school."

The man's eyebrows shot up. "Well now, is that a fact?"

"Yes, so you see, until things are settled—" She halted. "Would it be possible for me to leave my trunk here until I know where I'll be living?"

"Yes, ma'am. I'll see it's safe until"—he smiled wryly—"you need it."

"Thank you," Darcy said again, a bit tentatively. Something in the man's tone made her uneasy. Probably her imagination. Having come so far into this new environment, everything felt strange.

Braving the wind, carrying her suitcase and valise, she crossed the dusty street. Directly opposite the station house stood a weathered two-story with a wooden sign swinging over the entrance: "The Grand Hotel."

Not very grand, Darcy thought as she entered. The floor was bare, stained from tobacco juice that had missed the battered brass spittoons placed near several dilapidated chairs set at irregular angles around the lobby.

At the other end, louvered swinging doors led into the saloon, from which were emerging clouds of smoke as well as the sound of male voices, the clink of glasses, loud laughter. Even though it wasn't yet four o'clock, business seemed to be booming.

Looking straight ahead, she walked up to the registration desk. A bald-headed man in a boldly striped shirt, sleeves held back from his wrist with elastic bands, watched her approach speculatively. It occurred to her that perhaps this hotel didn't have many women guests. Maybe that was why he was eyeing her so curiously. Come to think of it, she hadn't seen any women since her arrival. Weren't there any female residents in this town?

The man gave her a long appraising look. "Yes, ma'am?"

"I would like a room, please." Darcy tried to sound assured, as if being alone in a strange town and acquiring a hotel room was not something unusual for her.

"For how long?"

"I'm not sure. For tonight at least." She felt sure that when she introduced herself to the chairman of the school board, he would tell her what accommodations had been made for her. The employment advertisement she'd answered had stated that living quarters would be provided. Until then she would have to put up with whatever was available. At the moment this was it.

The clerk peered over the counter. "Is that all of your luggage?"

"I left my trunk at the train station. Perhaps you can send someone over for it later?" She felt uncomfortable having to explain her circumstances to everyone. She drew herself up to her full five foot four and asked, "How much?"

"One dollar for the night. In advance."

Darcy drew a dollar out of her purse and handed it to him.

"Two if you want a bath. Fifty cents for extra hot water and towels," the clerk rattled off as he turned to get a key off a hook on the board behind him. He laid the key on the counter. "Number six. Third door to your left at the top of the stairs." He pointed a grubby index finger to a stairway.

Darcy went up the rickety steps and down a narrow, dark hall. At the door with the brass numeral six, she inserted the key in the lock and turned it, opened the door into a room about the size of their pantry at home. It contained a single iron posted bed, a straight chair, a washstand holding a chipped enamel pitcher and bowl. She walked across the creaky bare floor—which tilted slightly, as if it had been laid by a tipsy carpenter—to the window. She pushed aside thin curtains stiff with ingrained dust and looked out. The street below was deserted. Nobody seemed to be going about the business of the town. She suppressed a little shudder. Was this one of those legendary ghost towns of the West? What on earth had she got herself into?

She sat down gingerly on the side of the bed and sighed deeply. Suddenly a wave of loneliness swept over her. Tears threatened. She refused to give way to them. She couldn't appear at the meeting tonight red-nosed, swollen-eyed. This wouldn't do. She emptied her handbag on the bed in search of a hankie. Among the contents was the employment ad, which she had impulsively cut out of the newspaper and answered the week after she'd ended her engagement to Grady. She reread it now.

> *Needed immediately. Full-time teacher for grades one through eight in Juniper Junction, Kansas. Desperate.*

Desperate! Well, she was desperate, too.

With it another scrap of paper had fallen out. It was the crumpled tract she had absentmindedly tossed into her purse when she found it on her seat on the train. "You need Jesus," it reminded her. She replaced it in her purse and continued to sift through the small pile on the bed.

She noticed a small brown-paper package she didn't remember putting in her handbag. She unwrapped it and found a tiny ring box. She recognized it immediately. How had it got in here? Maybe softhearted Auntie Sadie, sympathetic to Grady, had placed it there. Folded around the little jewel box was a note written in a familiar boyish scrawl.

Dear Sweetheart,
I'm giving you back your ring. I don't want to be unengaged.
I meant it for keeps. I don't care what you say. Your aunt told
me you won't see me or talk to me, so I asked her to see that
you got this anyway. She says teachers' contracts are usually
just for a year. A lot can happen in a year. I could even lose the
election. I've loved you for a long time and I can't quit now.
Yours,
Grady

Too late, Grady. This is all your fault. Darcy opened her valise and tucked the ring box in one of the pockets, then groped in it for a bottle of rose water and glycerine to pat on her face. She was due to appear at the school board meeting tonight, and she had to look her best. Even if the position was only for one year. Only! Twelve months stretched out before her, full of unknowns. *Grady was right—a year is a long time. Anything can happen in a year.*

She felt tired yet tense. Tonight would be a totally new experience for her. The Baldwins were one of the pioneer families in a town her great-grandfather had practically built, and her uncle was a judge. Darcy was used to being liked, even envied a little. Facing a roomful of strangers who had employed her sight unseen to be their children's new teacher was unnerving.

At ten minutes to six she put on a fresh blouse, its ruffled collar standing up over the snug jacket of her suit. After dusting her face lightly with rice powder, she redid her hair, then studied her reflection in the cracked mirror over the washstand. She hoped she fit the image of a capable school-marm. She checked her lapel watch and took a deep breath. It was time to go.

She arrived at the town hall at 6:20 on the dot.

As she entered, she saw that a man on the stage was the same one behind the ticket counter at the train station. He must indeed be a member of the school board. Why hadn't he told her?

Aware of people's curious glances, she found a seat at the end of the second row. The gavel was pounded by a large, florid-faced man, and the meeting was called to order. Minutes of the last meeting were read. Among the list of topics that had been discussed was the urgent search for an elementary school teacher. Darcy straightened her shoulders and leaned forward, expecting at this point to be intro-duced. She swallowed over her dry throat. Her heart was thumping as she mentally prepared what she would say. She started to stand, when with a flourish the chairman ges-tured to a lean, bespectacled, middle-aged man sitting at the end of the stage and announced in a loud voice, "Mr. Marcus Manley, our town's newest citizen and the new elementary school teacher."

THREE

D arcy sat frozen, her gloved hands clenched in her lap. She stared at the five board members on the stage. What had happened to her application? Why hadn't she been notified? She sat there in a daze as applause sounded all around her. She hardly heard the few words of thanks Mr. Manley spoke.

After the meeting was adjourned, Darcy pulled herself together. She gathered her wits enough to decide to speak to the chairman, determined to get some explanation.

Darcy waited until he finished talking to a group of citizens. Then, with as much dignity as she could muster, she approached him. "Sir," she began politely. "I'm Darcy Welburne. There must be some mistake. I'm here—I mean, I've come to take the position you've just handed to that gentleman." She inclined her head toward Mr. Manley, who was now circled by people, possibly parents of the students he had been hired to teach.

Slowly the chairman made the connection and then turned beet red. "Yes, ma'am, and I'm Clyde Fenley, school board chairman." He stammered a bit. "I...I'm mighty sorry, Miss Welburne. Jest afore the meeting, Jake Henson, the train station manager, told me you'd come this afternoon. We sent you a letter telling you the position was filled. You must have left home afore our letter come. You see, Miss Welburne, Mr. Manley was known to several of the school board members and highly recommended. We got so many big fellas in the school, and menfolks seem to be better able to handle the older boys than a woman. Beg pardon, miss, but that's what tipped the scales. No offense. Your qualifications were jest fine. Yes siree. Now that you've already made the trip and if you're interested, they're in bad need of a schoolmarm over at Minersville. Had to close the school last year cuz the teacher quit. And they ain't had no one since. It's nigh on to seventy-five miles from here. Far as I know, they haven't filled the position yet. There's a train out of here at seven A.M. you can catch, makes a stop at Minersville." His tone was somehow not reassuring.

Darcy had too much pride to show what a blow this was. She accepted Mr. Fenley's explanation and suggestion as graciously as possible and somehow managed to leave the town hall with her composure intact.

But walking back to the hotel, she felt devastated. Having come so far, where else could she go? One thing she knew she could *not* do was go home. How Grady would gloat, and everyone else would be in a hurry to remind her they had all "told her so."

What could she do? Minersville, wherever that was, seemed to be her only option. Darcy had never felt so alone in her life.

By the time she reached the hotel, Darcy had made two resolutions. Discouraged and disheartened as she felt she refused to give up, go home. She had always been told she had spunk.

Maybe by spunk people actually meant hardheadedness. She realized she had acted impulsively. She had felt that she didn't need Grady, didn't need anyone. Now she felt ashamed at the prospect of facing him and the others.

For some reason she thought of the tract with the blunt assertion on its cover. Belatedly she realized she did need help. She did need Jesus. Brought up in a Bible-believing, churchgoing family, among people who prayed about everything from good weather for the annual Sunday school picnic to the outcome of an election, Darcy should have found asking for direction and help to be natural. But she felt too guilty. After all, she had rushed ahead, made her own plans without asking anybody. Look where that had got her. Miles from home and anyone she knew, without a job, without a clue as to what to do next.

Back at the hotel she climbed wearily up the steps and let herself into the room she had rented for the night. She shut and locked the door, then threw herself on her knees beside the bed.

Tears streaming down her face, Darcy leaned against the sagging mattress and prayed to God for help.

Finally Darcy got up, took off her hat and jacket. It may or may not have been an answer to prayer, but at least she had come to the conclusion that the only thing she could do was take Mr. Fenley's advice and go on to Minersville. How much worse could it be?

She contemplated the bed. Used to immaculate bedding, sheets scented with lavender, she felt finicky about getting into this one. Darcy spread her petticoat over the bed and the pillow and covered herself with her flannel nightgown and finally fell asleep.

She spent a hard night tossing and turning restlessly on the thin, lumpy mattress, catching snatches of sleep between the raucous sounds reaching her all night long from the saloon downstairs.

At the first gray light of dawn she got up. The train would arrive at 7:00 and leave again at 7:10, just time enough to load freight, take on passengers, if any. She had to be at the station. She couldn't miss it. The thought of spending another night here made her shudder.

She washed as best she could in the tepid water remaining in the pitcher on the washstand. She applied her rose water liberally, brushed her hair, put it up, then got into her jacket and pinned on her hat. She would try to get a cup of coffee in the hotel dining room. She repacked her toiletries in her valise, picked up her suitcase, and went downstairs. The desk clerk had been replaced by a skinny young fellow with a shock of red hair, and a face so freckled that it looked like a polka-dot pattern with two bright-green eyes. He blinked a couple of times at Darcy's question about the possibility of a cup of coffee, then stuttered, "Breakfast don't get served for another half an hour, but Cook's here, miss. Mebbe you could get a mug if it's made."

He used his thumb to indicate the door that opened into the kitchen. Darcy looked in the direction he pointed and saw an Oriental man who was ranting in Chinese as he gestured with a spatula to a small, thin man wearing a shirt and vest and a soiled apron. She approached them, and at her request for coffee the second man turned and stared in surprise. She smiled, applying her charm, which usually worked well for her. "I have to catch the seven o'clock train," she explained.

"Well, I dunno—," he replied and glanced at the Chinese man, who looked blank.

"Coffee?" Darcy repeated, making a motion of holding a cup and sipping.

The cook grinned and nodded. "Sure, missee." He bustled over to the huge, black stove, returning with a thick, white mug of steaming coffee. It was scalding hot and so bitter, it made her eyes blink. However, it served the purpose of jolting her foggy brain to full alertness. Gathering up her luggage, she left the misnamed hotel and made her way along the silent street to the train station.

As she sat on the bench on the station platform, waiting for the train, Darcy prayed. From memory she recited what she had heard so often: "Everything works together for good to those who love the Lord and are called to his purpose." It had always been said by Grandma Bee, echoed by her mother and aunts, when anything went wrong. She found it strangely comforting. What more could go wrong?

Just then she heard the train whistle and saw the locomotive, with its stream of smoke, rounding the bend of the track.

With a sinking feeling, she watched her trunk being put back into the baggage car. In another ten minutes she was sitting on a rigid coach seat, rushing through a desolate landscape toward another unfamiliar destination. What awaited her there was anyone's guess. Maybe she should look over the teacher's information list that Mr. Fenley had given her the night before. She unfolded it.

The Minersville School Board Rules for Teachers

1. Each day fill lamps, clean chimneys.
2. Bring a bucket of water and a scuttle of coal for each day's session.
3. Make pupils' pens, whittle nibs according to each one's taste, ability.
4. Men teachers may have one evening each week for courting purposes, or two evenings if they attend church regularly.
5. After the ten-hour school day, teachers should spend the remaining time reading the Bible or other good books.
6. Women teachers who marry or engage in unseemly conduct will be dismissed.

7. Teachers should lay aside a goodly sum each payday to provide for his or her declining years so that he or she will not become a burden on the community.
8. Any teacher who smokes, uses any kind of spirits, frequents pool or public halls, or gets shaved in a barber shop will give reason to suspect his worth, intention, integrity, and honesty.
9. The teacher who performs his or her labor faithfully and without fault for five years will be given an increase of twenty-five cents per week in his or her pay, contingent upon the local school board's approval.

If Darcy hadn't been depressed before reading this, she was now. What a list of rules to look forward to for the next year. She wasn't sure she could live up to any of them—except possibly number 8! Even a year's contract would seem like a sentence to hard labor in prison. Again she sent a heartfelt prayer heavenward. *"Please,* Lord, rescue me."

"Would you like an apple, dearie?" a pleasant voice asked, jerking Darcy back from her dismal thoughts to the present. The speaker was a motherly-looking lady sitting across the aisle from her. She was smiling and holding out a shiny red Jonathan.

The woman offering it had twinkling blue eyes, curly gray hair circling a round, rosy face. She reminded Darcy of the illustration of Pegotty, the nurse in her favorite Dickens novel, *David Copperfield*.

"Why, thank you," Darcy said gratefully.

The woman took a blue checkered napkin from the wicker basket on the seat beside her and passed it over along with the apple. "They're very juicy. Just picked yesterday in my brother's orchard. I've been visiting there for the past week. I'm Alberta Mason. But everyone calls me Bertie."

Darcy nodded and introduced herself. Then she took a bite of the apple. "Mmm," she murmured appreciatively. "This is really good."

The woman looked pleased that Darcy was enjoying it.

Darcy finished the apple, wiped her mouth and hands on the napkin, and handed it back to Bertie. "That was delicious. Thank you very much."

"You're more than welcome, dearie. I'm a seasoned traveler, you might say. I always take a little something along in case of unexpected delays that happen along the way. Even though I plan to take lunch at the Harvey House in Emporia. And that will be a treat," Bertie said, whipping out some yarn and beginning to crochet what appeared to be an afghan square. "But it's nice to fall in with a pleasant companion to whittle away the traveling time, which can get tedious on a long trip." She took a few more stitches, then glanced again at Darcy and commented, "I noticed you were traveling all alone and looked. . .well, kinda downhearted. Away from home for the first time, are you, dearie?"

Because of the sudden lump in her throat, Darcy could only nod.

Bertie clucked sympathetically.

Soon Darcy began to confide what had happened to her at Juniper Junction. Bertie listened intently.

Darcy had prayed for rescue, never dreaming it would come in the form of a plump fellow passenger. But she was to discover that God is full of surprises.

FOUR

Before long Darcy found herself pouring out her tale of woe to this stranger with kind blue eyes. As she recounted her dismay about the job she had expected to fill disappearing in front of her eyes, Bertie kept nodding and making appropriate sympathetic sounds.

Finally tears Darcy could no longer hold back rolled down her cheeks. "I'm sorry," she said, sniffing. "I didn't mean to burden you with my personal problems." She took out her handkerchief and dabbed at her eyes. "At least I have another job waiting for me."

"And where is that, dearie?"

"The school board chairman told me they need a teacher in Minersville."

At this Bertie gasped. She patted her chest with one hand as though she were about to have a heart attack. "Oh my, not Minersville! He wouldn't have sent you there. I do declare!"

Alarmed, Darcy asked, "Why? What's the matter with Minersville?"

"Oh, dearie me," Bertie said, shaking her head. "Minersville is...well, it's back of beyond, the other side of nowhere." She fanned herself with her napkin. "It's in the desert, a ghost town, practically. The mines ran out years ago, and it's just some ramshackle buildings and a few people holding on for no real purpose, that somehow...Oh no, dearie, I don't think you should go there." She paused and took a long breath. "Are they expecting you to come? Did you sign a contract?"

"No, but if I don't go there, I have nowhere else to go, no job at all. And I can't go back home."

"And why is that, dearie?"

Darcy had not ever imagined telling someone she'd just met about Grady. But Bertie had such warmth, seemed so concerned and interested, that Darcy gave her the whole dismal story.

"He sounds like a fine young man," Bertie commented, putting her head to one side and regarding Darcy thoughtfully.

"He is," Darcy assured her. "Yes, of course he is, but I simply had to put my foot down. I couldn't bear to marry a man in politics. And isn't it better to have been honest with him before we went ahead and got married?"

"Oh my, yes, dearie. Better by far, than for both of you to be miserable. As Scripture says, 'A contentious wife is a

constant dripping.' I've seen enough of life to know nag-
ging'll ruin a marriage, that's for sure. If you weren't happy,
neither would your young man be."

"So you see, I can't go back home now. Whatever
Minersville is like, I have to stick it out, at least for a year,"
Darcy said with more conviction than she felt. The look on
Bertie's face at the mention of Minersville had sent splin-
ters of apprehension all through her. But what else could
she do?

Bertie tapped her pink cheek with one finger and
frowned as if she were thinking very hard. After a few minutes she set her mouth in a firm line.

"On such short acquaintance, maybe I shouldn't be
giving you advice. But let me tell you about my niece
Annie."

What Bertie's niece could possibly have to do with her
present dilemma, Darcy had no idea. But at this point she
was willing to listen to any suggestion.

"Well, have you ever heard of Fred Harvey?" Bertie
began.

Darcy shook her head. "No. Should I have?"

"Not unless you traveled through the West in the old
days." Bertie rolled her eyes to indicate something unknown
to the uninitiated. "Well, I did, following my husband, who
was a mining engineer, from place to place. It was no picnic
in the park, believe you me. And at the time I had two small
children along. Back east the trains provided good customer
services. They had dining cars, Pullman sleeping cars. But
out here? My, no. Railroads traveling out west went through

hundreds of miles of open country. There were no restaurants, no clean hotels where a traveler could get rest and refreshment. Most of the stops were mining camps, cattle pens, or army outposts. It was mighty dreadful. You had to develop an iron stomach to eat a bite. What was available mostly was greasy meat, canned beans, biscuits that tasted like alkali dust, and tea that tasted like it was brewed from sagebrush." Bertie gave her recital dramatic impact, then ended it with a flourish. "That is, until Fred Harvey."

"Who was he?"

"Who was he? You only have to say the name west of the Mississippi to get an answer. He was an elegant, fastidious Englishman with refined tastes and a brilliant business mind. He saw a need and filled it, beautifully and successfully. At each major railroad station, he opened restaurants that served the first decent meals any westbound train traveler had eaten." Bertie paused, waiting for some reaction from Darcy. When it didn't come immediately, she went on. "There's one in Emporia, and we'll be there in two hours, and you can see for yourself."

"But Minersville is the next stop. The conductor told me they only stop long enough to take on water and"— Darcy finished weakly—"let off any passengers whose destination it is."

Bertie leaned forward and patted Darcy's hand.

"That's just why I'm telling you all this. *Before* we get to Minersville and before you get off."

"I don't understand. Telling me what? That if I get off at Minersville, I'll be missing a great meal?"

"Land sakes, no, child! More than that. A chance to become a Harvey Girl."

"A Harvey Girl?"

"Yes. Fred Harvey was just as particular about the staff who served the meals as he was of the food itself, which was the finest, the freshest, and as gourmet as that of any exclusive eastern restaurant. He began hiring young women. And he was very particular about the applicants. He established a strict set of rules that his restaurants continue to follow. Harvey Girls have to be attractive in appearance, have to have graduated from high school, and have to exhibit refined speech and good manners. If they meet those standards, they are accepted. They have to sign a contract to remain for six to nine months or a year and agree to follow to the letter his instructions. They have to obey employee rules, go to work wherever a Harvey House is located, not marry within the time of their employment. If they agree, they go through an intense training program before being assigned to one of the Harvey House restaurants situated all along the railroad line. Everything is taken care of for them. They stay in dormitories, two girls to a room, their room and board is free, plus they receive salaries and tips, which are usually generous. They have one full day a week off and half days on Sundays to attend the church service of their choice."

Bertie paused again, sat back, and assumed a waiting attitude.

Darcy frowned. "So what has all this to do with me?"

"I think you should consider applying to become a Harvey Girl. Believe me, dearie, it would be far, far better than what you're heading into in Minersville."

"Better? Being a waitress instead of a teacher?"

"Being a *Harvey Girl.*" Bertie let her emphasis sink in for a moment before continuing. "You see, dearie, my niece, the one I was telling you about? She has been a Harvey Girl for the past year and a half in Emporia—and loves it. If you stay on the train until we get there, we can go in and have dinner and she can tell you about it herself. What do you think of that?"

"But what about my train ticket?" Darcy said, almost to herself.

"Of course, it's your decision, dearie. But I don't think you'll be sorry if you decide to pass up Minersville and go on with me to Emporia." She paused. "When the conductor comes through again, shall I tell him that there will be two reservations for lunch in the dining room? The conductor always telegraphs ahead so the staff at Harvey House knows how many to expect."

Darcy sat very still, nearly motionless, deep in thought as the train traveled ever nearer to Minersville. The alternative to getting out there was—becoming a waitress? A waitress in a busy restaurant catering to train passengers? She had never heard of these Harvey House restaurants Bertie described. Much less considered working in one as a waitress. She thought of her mother, of Auntie Sadie, and especially of Aunt Maude—admittedly a bit of a snob—and Uncle Henry and all her status-conscious relatives. What would they think? They didn't even know any women who worked outside their home. That is, except for women who were forced by dire necessity to support a family. Being a teacher was different—it was an accepted role. A teacher was a respected member of the community. But a waitress was classed with housemaids or laundresses. However, the way Bertie had put it, being a Harvey Girl was a superior kind of job.

Well, she'd already gone out on a limb by leaving Willowdale; should she take another chance? Even on this short acquaintance she liked and trusted Bertie. Still, Darcy was unsure.

"We'll be coming into Emporia in a couple of hours. Annie knows I'm coming today. She'll be expecting me and will seat us at her table." Bertie beamed, her blue eyes twinkling. "I know you're going to take to her. Like all the Harvey Girls, she's got a winning personality and makes you feel like royalty when you're being served."

A thread of excitement ran all through Darcy's body. Her spirit, which had been so low, took an upward bounce. What an unexpected event meeting Bertie had been. What a startling idea she had presented to her. Darcy had prayed for the Lord to rescue her. As he often did, he was answering her prayer in a way she would never have imagined. The important thing was to recognize that answer when it came.

"All right, I'll do it," she said.

"Good girl!" exclaimed Bertie. "I don't think you'll be sorry."

FIVE

When Darcy and her new friend got off the train in Emporia, the first thing they saw on the station platform was a newlywed couple surrounded by a group of well-wishers seeing them off on their honeymoon. As she heard the shouts of good wishes and watched the bride toss her bouquet, Darcy had a bad moment. That could have been her and Grady, if only . . .

A twinge of regret gripped her. Had she been too quick to give up her chance of being a bride? Her chance for happiness, security? Had she been entirely too reckless?

"Come along, dearie," Bertie said, taking her arm. "We only have an hour and forty-five minutes before the train leaves." Darcy remembered Grandma Bee saying, "What's too late to mend is too late for tears." Well, it *was* too late.

She had taken her stand and Grady had had his chance. Now was the time to move on to whatever awaited her.

They walked the short distance to the restaurant and entered the dining room, a spacious area with shining mahogany counters, gleaming, chrome-plated coffee urns, sparkling crystal glassware. Tables placed at comfortable distances from each other were covered with white linen cloths. At each serving station a young woman, neatly dressed in black with white collar and cuffs and a crisp bib apron, stood waiting to serve.

Bertie told Darcy, "The conductor on the incoming train goes through the cars asking people where they wish to eat, in the dining room"—she lowered her voice to add, "which is more expensive"—"or in the lunchroom, where the menu is à la carte. Then the information is wired ahead so that everything can be prepared. Meals are ready to be served, the coffee is freshly made, all is perfectly timed." She squeezed Darcy's arm. "There's Annie." She inclined her head to a pretty young woman coming toward them with a big smile.

Annie greeted her aunt affectionately and showed them to a table. Their coffee cups were immediately filled while Bertie made the introductions quietly. Then Annie took their order, telling them what the specialty of the day was. Everything was served smoothly, with no sense of rush, even though Bertie confided that the girls were expert in timing so that no passenger ever was in danger of missing his or her train. Darcy had ordered chicken, and Bertie veal cutlets with applesauce. After Darcy's first bite Bertie asked, "Now is that good or what?"

"Wonderful!" Darcy replied.

Bertie smiled with satisfaction. "Didn't I tell you? As fine as anything you would get in any of the best restaurants in St. Louis or New Orleans, don't you think?"

Darcy had not experienced either one, but she was sure Bertie was right. They had just finished when Annie came for their dessert choice. Soon apricot pie was set before them, and their cups refilled with steaming coffee.

When they were finished eating, Annie took away their plates, then came back, saying, "I have permission to visit with you, Aunt Bertie. We can go into the hotel lounge."

When they were settled at one end of the lobby, Bertie told Annie that Darcy was interested in applying for a position as a Harvey Girl. Was there any possibility of getting an interview?

Annie gave Darcy a long look. "If you don't mind hard work and long hours, you'll love it." She paused, then said, "You're in luck—two girls left last week and we're short-handed here. Miss Viola Colby, who does the hiring, is in Topeka today interviewing. Wait here and let me check with my head waitress, Miss Casey, and see if she can set up an appointment for you."

Darcy felt a thrill of anticipation, not unmixed with a little nervousness. Things were moving so fast, it seemed unreal. It was all so uncanny—meeting with Bertie, the fact that she had a niece who worked as a Harvey Girl, and the discovery that the restaurant was now hiring.

When Annie returned, she was accompanied by a dignified young woman dressed in black with a high white collar like those of the waitresses but without the apron.

After introductions were exchanged, Miss Casey sat down and began to interview Darcy.

"I'm afraid I've had no real experience waiting tables," Darcy offered a little timidly.

Miss Casey made a dismissive gesture and said, "All the better, actually. Harvey Girls have to learn the system used in all our restaurants. That's why there is such a long and rigorous training period. Thirty days. Time to drill every detail required into a girl's mind before she is put to work." Miss Casey took a small notebook out of her pocket and made a few notations in it, then repeated Annie's comment.

"You're in luck, Miss Welburne. Our manager is in Topeka today and tomorrow to interview applicants. I'll give you a railroad pass, and you can take the afternoon train to see her. If all goes well and she approves, you may be hired and start your training right away." Miss Casey stood up. She gave Darcy an encouraging smile that changed her rather severe expression, and held out her hand. "I hope you'll soon be one of our Harvey Girls."

"I think she likes you," Annie said after Miss Casey left. "I'm sure she'll put in a good word for you with Miss Colby!"

Bertie squeezed Darcy's arm. "What did I tell you?"

Darcy left Bertie and Annie to continue their visit and catch up on family news, and hurried to the train station. There she arranged to have her trunk taken off the train and held for her in the baggage claim until she knew what the result of her interview might be. Her heart was pounding. What if this turned out to be a wild-goose chase? Compared with the teaching post in Minersville, however, this seemed a better choice.

Before boarding the train to Topeka, Darcy wrote out a message for the telegrapher at the station to send to her family.

Changed plans. Checking out new job opportunity in Topeka. Further information to follow.

When she knew how things had turned out, she would write them a letter.

Bertie arrived at the station just before her own train was due to depart. She gave Darcy a hug. "Good-bye and God bless. I'm sure all will go well for you."

Darcy thanked Bertie for everything, but Bertie just shook her head. "The Lord's the one to thank. He engineers our circumstances."

Was that true? Or was meeting Bertie just a coincidence? Darcy didn't think so. However it had all come about, she was clutching a railroad pass to Topeka in her hand, on her way to a whole new unscheduled adventure.

PART
TWO

SIX

At the Harvey headquarters in Topeka, Darcy was ushered into the office where Miss Colby, the personnel manager, interviewed applicants. Darcy felt rather as if she had been called into the principal's office in high school.

Miss Colby, a handsome woman in her mid-forties, greeted Darcy pleasantly. "Please be seated, Miss Welburne." She gestured to a chair opposite her desk. "So you want to be a Harvey Girl?" she asked, smiling.

Without waiting for an answer, she asked Darcy several questions, then explained what the qualifications were for becoming a Harvey Girl and what would be expected of her if she signed up. "We usually ask ourselves certain questions about a young woman who applies for the job. Does she have the brains and ability to follow directions? Is she dependable and responsible and sensible? Is she teachable? That's the most important question. Harvey House has very set rules of service that have to be followed exactly, with no innovations."

Miss Colby looked directly at Darcy, as if to see how she was taking all this so far. Then she continued. "I interview many young women who think they want to work for us, but I find that just as many have no idea what we expect of those we hire. So I always feel it necessary to outline our requirements before we go any further. A high school education is required, preferably church membership, a neat, attractive appearance, a courteous manner, good grammar, nice speaking voice. These are fairly obvious qualities any employer might look for in someone who will be dealing with the public. However, Harvey House has other requirements that are just as important."

Miss Colby paused. "Vulgarity of any kind will not be tolerated. A willingness to work and learn the Harvey system, which is unique and very exacting, is imperative. Mr. Harvey counted on the Harvey Girls to represent the whole enterprise to the people who would visit his restaurants. Make the best impression. Therefore he laid out a very stringent set of rules that must be followed."

Darcy listened with a sinking heart, tensing herself for whatever was next.

"You must agree to learn the Harvey system, follow all instructions to the letter, obey the employee rules, accept whatever location to which you're assigned or at which you're needed on short notice. We require you to sign a choice of contracts, from six months to a year in duration. There is no use in our spending so much time training a girl with a guaranteed time of employment that is any less. Also, you must agree not to change your marital status for the length of your contract. There is no fraternizing with male employees of the Harvey staff or socializing with customers. Do you have any problem with that?"

"No problem," Darcy answered firmly.

After the disastrous ending of her romance with Grady, Darcy had no intention of getting involved with anyone. Not for a long time. Maybe not ever! Her disappointment in Grady still hurt.

Miss Colby's crisp voice broke into her momentary distraction. "I see here on your application that you're pretty far from home, Miss Welburne. Any chance of your getting homesick and wanting to leave us before you fulfill your contract?"

"None at all," Darcy answered unwaveringly. "I'm prepared to make a one-year commitment." Her family and friends did not expect her back in Willowdale for at least a year. However this waitressing turned out, she could certainly manage that.

"You must satisfactorily complete the thirty-day training period before you are placed in any of the restaurants. During that time you will not be paid; however, your room and board is provided."

Miss Colby waited to see some reaction. There was none immediately. So she continued. "Harvey Girls live in dormitories either above the restaurant or in an adjacent building. Room, board, uniforms are all provided. The salary is thirty-five dollars a month."

Darcy's ears perked up at that. A Harvey Girl's salary would be more than what she would have made as a teacher. As a waitress, she would also receive tips from restaurant customers. With food, lodging, and clothing taken care of, being a Harvey Girl would be better than the life she would have had as a teacher. Darcy began to feel more cheerful.

"Railroad passes to anywhere on the routes are available for trips home or for the annual vacation," Miss Colby concluded. "Do you understand and agree to all the Harvey requirements?"

Darcy nodded. "Yes, I understand and agree."

Miss Colby smiled. "I think you're exactly the type Harvey House looks for. Of course, we never know until a young woman is put to the test."

"I'd certainly like to try," Darcy said.

"Very well. After you sign, we'll get you started. You can begin your training tomorrow. The thirty days is sometimes expanded. It depends on a young woman's aptitude and how quickly she learns. Until we are satisfied that you know the Harvey system by heart, we don't send you out."

Miss Colby opened a folder on her desk and took out a contract and handed it to Darcy. "Sign in the appropriate line."

After Darcy signed, Miss Colby took it, examined it briefly, then slid it back into the folder. She stood up, opened a file cabinet drawer, and placed the folder inside.

"Let's go. First I'll take you to the dormitory, get you settled. Come along."

Darcy followed Miss Colby down a long corridor, outside, and up a flight of stairs that led to the dormitory above the restaurant.

"Two girls share each room. We expect everyone to get along by being flexible, unselfish, generous. Everyone helps everyone else."

Miss Colby opened the door to a room with two iron beds, two chests of drawers, and a wardrobe. Everything was neat, and very few personal items were on display.

"You'll be rooming with Dorothy Mills, one of our old girls who'll show you the ropes. She's very nice. I'm sure you'll like her."

Darcy had never shared a bedroom with anyone. A picture of her spacious room at home, with its ruffled curtains, the maple four-poster bed, the little desk at the window, came to mind. But not with nostalgia. She was already feeling a stir of excitement. She was on the brink of an entirely new experience and eager to begin it.

Next she was taken to find her size in the regulation uniform. This was an ankle-length, plain black dress, of which the high neck and long sleeves had a stiff white collar and cuffs. Over this was worn a white bib apron. Then she was fitted with high-top black shoes to be worn with black stockings. Her hair was to be worn simply, drawn back from the face, no pompadour or crimping, and into a knot at the nape of the neck, then covered with a hair net.

The first part of her initiation as a Harvey Girl had happened so quickly that Darcy was unprepared for the jolting reality of the rigorous training period that started the very next morning.

Her roommate, Dorothy, awakened her at five-thirty, told her to get dressed in her uniform and report to the kitchen area at six. The thirty days had begun.

It was like the first day of school all over again, Darcy thought excitedly. Once in her uniform, Darcy looked in the mirror and adored the costume. The black dress and crisp apron showed off her slim figure and tiny waist. The simple hairdo was becoming to her oval face, enhanced her golden-maple brown hair and dark eyes. This was fun, like playing a role in a school play. If she was just able to learn her lines!

Several hours later Darcy had to reverse her first notion that waitressing was fun. The training she had been told about began at once, and it was thorough. Darcy had never had to take orders or endure much discipline at home. Here everything was about obeying commands and toeing the mark. The trainees were instructed to watch everything the experienced waitresses did.

The first morning, the head waitress in Topeka, Miss Nelson, who was in charge of training the new employees, informed them, "We put our girls on the job immediately. Not actually serving but beginning to learn. You'll start in the lunchroom. You'll have to observe everything, all the details—that's the important thing which makes all the difference. You'll soon get an idea of what is expected of a Harvey Girl."

What was expected was a full day of undivided attention. Harvey Girls did not hover over the customers but stood at a respectful distance, alert to fill whatever need anyone had. There was hardly time to worry about being homesick or fraternizing with members of the male staff or socializing with the customers. Darcy mentally rolled her eyes at such a suggestion. Her days were too busy with learning the system, and at night she was too weary to do anything but fall into bed, exhausted. There was so much to learn and absorb.

Certain things were unique to the Harvey system and had to be done exactly. Each detail of serving had to be memorized so that it would be second nature in a restaurant filled with hungry customers. The cup code, for instance.

The cup code had to become automatic. A cup upright in its saucer meant coffee; a cup turned upside down meant hot tea; a cup upside down and tilted against its saucer meant iced tea; one upside down and away from its saucer meant milk. Another variation: if the handle of the cup was pointed to six o'clock, it meant coffee; to high noon, black tea; three o'clock, green tea; nine o'clock, orange pekoe; if the cup was removed, it meant an order for milk.

Food preparation was as precise for the kitchen staff as was the serving ritual for the waitresses. Everything had to be fresh. Orange juice had to be squeezed each morning, not made the night before and stored in a refrigerator. Ice cream was made with all the best and freshest ingredients, including eggs and cream. Fruits and vegetables, chickens, eggs were purchased locally. Harvey restaurants took enormous pride in the freshness of everything served. Huge bulk-storage refrigerators held salmon from San Francisco, celery from Michigan, honeydew, Persian melons, apples, pears, lemons, oranges from California, French cheese such as Camembert, Portuguese sardines, and Kansas beef.

A Harvey Girl was always busy, even when not serving. Between rounds of train customers, she had to completely clean her station, "up to the standard." That meant everything: tables cleared, used dishes and silverware carried away to be washed, her station left spotless and gleaming, ready to be set again for the next arrival of passengers.

It seemed a hard, unrelenting pace. But Darcy refused to be discouraged. She wasn't about to give up before she started. She reminded herself what the alternative might have been in Minersville. She had "set her hand to the plow," and she had no intention of looking back. She was determined to become the best Harvey Girl possible.

At last she successfully completed the thirty-day training period and was sent to Emporia to work.

SEVEN

OCTOBER 1903

U pon Darcy's arrival back in Emporia, the head waitress there, Miss Casey, told Darcy she was to replace Annie, who had been transferred to Santa Fe.

Darcy felt a pang of alarm. She had counted on Bertie's niece to help as she started her new job. Although the Harvey House training had been so thorough, she was still nervous. What if she couldn't remember everything she'd learned or forgot one of the Harvey rules?

Miss Casey gave her a requisition slip for additional uniforms and aprons, and the key to her room. "You'll be staying with Clementine Miller, who's been with us for nearly a year. I'm sure you'll get along just fine. We start our new girls out in the lunchroom until they're ready to serve in the dining room. You'll begin tomorrow, six o'clock sharp."

Assuming a confidence she did not feel, Darcy bundled her baggage up the steps to the waitresses' dormitory.

She found her assigned room and had just raised her hand to knock at the door when it flew open. Startled, Darcy took a step back.

Framed in the doorway was a rosy-cheeked young woman with reddish blond hair, a scattering of golden freckles over a turned-up nose, and the widest, friendliest grin Darcy had ever seen.

"Hello! You must be my new roomie," she greeted Darcy. "Annie moved out day before yesterday. Gone to New Mexico. Lucky girl! But the bed's all made and the closet's cleaned out, ready for you. I'm Clementine Miller. Call me Clemmie. Come on in." She easily lifted Darcy's suitcase and carried it inside, motioning for her to follow.

Darcy picked up her valise and walked into the room they were to share. She took a good look at her roommate. Clemmie was a strong, healthy-looking young woman. Darcy recalled Miss Colby mentioning the fact that many of the Harvey Girls came from farm families, preferring the job to farm chores. Within the next few minutes Darcy learned this was true of Clementine. She told Darcy she had been born and raised on her family's farm in Arkansas. She left to come west seeking adventure and romance.

Clemmie dimpled. "So far, no romance. But I like it a whole lot more than feeding chickens, gathering eggs, milking the cows, and slopping the hogs. I wanted something different than what I've been doing since I was five or six."

As she talked, Clemmie helped Darcy put away her belongings in the large wardrobe, showed her the bureau that had been emptied for her, all the while giving her the rundown on the other girls working at this Harvey House. Darcy could tell right away that Clemmie did not have a mean bone in her body. She said nothing catty or detrimental about anyone she described.

She was so warm and friendly, Darcy felt comfortable with her at once. Comfortable enough to confess, "I'm a little scared. Afraid I'll make some awful mistake and get fired."

Clemmie brushed away that suggestion. "Don't be. No need to be. All of us felt that way to begin with, but the other girls are really helpful and look out for the new ones. Someone will cover for you if you forget something. So don't worry. Before long it'll be easy as pie."

Never having been much at pie baking or managing a good crust, Darcy did not find that very reassuring. But Clemmie's attitude was catching and Darcy began to feel better. As the two chatted, getting acquainted, Clemmie talked about her family and showed Darcy pictures of them, which she had lined up on a bookshelf over her bed.

"Three brothers, Tom, Luke, Seth; two younger sisters, Edie and Mayme. They both want to be Harvey Girls when they grow up, like their big sister." She winked. "When I go home, they put on a cap and apron and play at being Harvey

Girls." She paused. "I guess they *did* tell you we get railroad passes for vacations and visits home, didn't they?"

Darcy nodded, thinking that she would hardly take advantage of that. Not only was Willowdale a very long train trip from here, but her family would not approve of the fact that she was working as a waitress, not a teacher.

"Of course, those of us that come from farm families get special leaves in spring and fall. To help with planting and harvesting. Mostly I help Mom do the cooking for all the extra help Pa hires."

She seemed about to ask Darcy about her family, when suddenly she looked at the clock on the bedside table and jumped. "I'd better scoot. We're supposed to be at our stations a half hour before the train is scheduled in. So make yourself at home; help yourself to anything you see." She made a sweeping gesture of the room. "The bathroom's down the hall. You'll have it to yourself during the dinner hour because we'll all be gone serving. And if you want anything to read, I've got back issues of the *Ladies' Home Gazette.* My mom sends it to me. I'm reading a serial—real scary, and romantic too."

As she talked, Clemmie tied on her starched white apron, adjusted the collar of her black dress, and stuffed her riotous curls into a hair net. At the door she said, "See you later." She went out, then popped her head back inside, saying, "I'm glad you're here, Darcy. It's going to be great having you as a roommate. Bye for now!" And with a wave she was gone.

Almost right away the two became friends, and the longer they knew each other, the deeper and stronger the friendship grew. Clemmie was so natural, outgoing, and openhearted. In a matter of days she told Darcy everything there was to know about herself.

Darcy met and liked the other girls too. There didn't seem to be any competition among them, nor the jealousy she had sometimes encountered back in Willowdale among some of her girlfriends. Being pretty and popular had sometimes been a problem. Being Judge Roscoe's niece had also been a liability. Among the Harvey Girls all that mattered was how well you did your work. That's what earned you respect.

She and Clemmie shared everything—laments about sore feet, complaints about cranky customers, as well as confidences. Clemmie had a great sense of humor, and laughter was the oil that made some of the rough times smooth. Darcy began to feel that Clemmie was the best friend she had ever made.

Clemmie seemed to have no secrets. She was open and honest about everything. Even about her reasons for becoming a Harvey Girl. Much as she loved her family, she confessed that for her, anything had sounded better than remaining on the farm.

It seemed easy and natural for Clemmie to tell Darcy anything. It made Darcy feel somewhat guilty not to be that forthcoming. Eventually she did tell Clemmie about breaking her engagement and why. However, one thing Darcy could not bring herself to tell Clemmie was that she was hiding her job from her family. She knew Clemmie would not understand how they would feel about her working as a waitress. Especially since Clemmie felt that becoming a Harvey Girl was a step up in the world.

Clemmie and some of the other more experienced waitresses had rescued her a couple of times. Miss Casey too, with just a lift of her eyebrow or a barely noticeable hand gesture, signaled in time to keep her from making a huge mistake.

Mixing up an order or forgetting the cup code and serving a diner tea instead of coffee, or switching a dessert choice to the wrong customer at the wrong table—none of these near-disasters were serious, and after recovering from her embarrassment, Darcy could even laugh about them.

As the weeks passed Darcy grew better at her job. Actually, Darcy came to love her life as a Harvey Girl. The more proficient she became, the more she enjoyed it. She still sometimes had the feeling she was acting a part on the stage. Being a Harvey Girl was so drastically different from her life in Willowdale or from anything she had ever imagined before.

She must have played her role very well, because after the first week in November she was awarded the prize for the most improved new waitress: a box of chocolates.

She rushed upstairs to share it with her roommate.

"You really deserve this more than me, Clemmie," she said as she opened the box and held it out for her to choose a piece. "You're the one who has helped me, teaching me all the special tricks and coaching me."

"Oh, go on! You've caught on faster than a lot of new girls. Besides, I won a box last summer. It's only fair to share the glory," Clemmie said, grinning and taking a bite. "Mmm, caramel nut. My favorite."

Darcy helped herself to a piece, thinking of all the boxes of candy she'd received from beaux back home. This box meant more than any of those. This one she'd earned by her own hard work. That made all the difference.

EIGHT

Darcy never meant to deceive. It all started with the telegram she sent her family when she was on her way for her interview in Topeka. When she was immediately hired and started her training, she had no time to write an explanatory letter about her change of occupations. So she had sent a second telegram simply stating that she was working in Topeka, that another letter would follow.

However, the letter that was to follow was put off for weeks. After she returned to Emporia as a full-fledged Harvey Girl, Darcy was kept busy in her new job. But not that busy. The real reason why she procrastinated was because she knew what her family's reaction would be. Her mother would be horrified, Auntie Sadie shocked, and most of all, Aunt Maude and Uncle Henry would be mortified that a niece of theirs, someone in their social position, had stooped to the job of waitressing in what they thought of as the Wild West.

Still, it had to be done. She could not put it off any longer. They'd be worried sick not to hear from her in so many weeks. So she finally made herself sit down and write this long postponed letter.

> *Dearest Mama, Auntie Sadie, Aunt Maude,*
> *and Uncle Henry,*
> *When I arrived in Juniper Junction, I discovered that the teaching post I assumed I would have was already filled, the male teacher already settled in. The chairman of the school board was kind enough to recommend another position to me that remained unfilled.*

Here Darcy stopped writing, wondering how she would explain the drastic change of events and occupation. She'd always been good at composition in school, using her imagination sometimes to embellish facts and enhance her subject matter. Almost without thinking, Darcy put this talent to use. Dipping her pen in the inkwell, she began again.

> *I find the new position very challenging and interesting.*

That was true enough. She didn't need to outline the exact nature of her job, did she?

> *I am rooming with a delightful girl, Clemmie Miller, who is most congenial, and we get along really well. She has lived here for nearly a year and is helping me get settled and intro-ducing me to people.*

Darcy stopped again, wondering how to continue.

She sings in the choir of a local church and has asked me to attend services with her next Sunday.

There! That ought to please and satisfy every member of her family.

You can write and mail me packages to general delivery here.

Before signing and sealing the letter, she added,

I know you will be relieved to know how well situated I am, how much I like my work, and that I have made good friends. I am not at all sorry about my decisions—any of them.

That should take care of the Grady issue, Darcy thought as she continued writing.

I believe this will be a wonderful learning experience and that this coming year will prove to be the best of my life so far. Please don't worry about me. I assure you I am in very good health and happily enjoying my new surroundings, new friends. This is all a great adventure.

As she addressed the envelope, Darcy prided herself that although she had skirted around the facts, given no exact details, there was nothing untrue about anything she had written.

Then why did she still feel guilty? She closed her eyes for a minute, picturing the Beehive's front porch shadowed by wisteria vines. There Grandma Bee and Darcy's mother and aunts sat on rush-seated rockers in the long afternoons doing needlework, returning the deferential greetings of neighbors as they passed by. Afterward discussing each one, not always in complimentary terms. Aunt Maude in particular always had something to say about everyone. Their clothes, their husbands, their housekeeping, their cooking, their children, their position in Willowdale society. Darcy winced, remembering how she had listened and sometimes even joined in, making comments that were just as critical. It made her ashamed that she had used her wit in such ways. She realized she had changed since she left Willowdale, became a Harvey Girl. Here such gossip wouldn't be tolerated. Here everyone was accepted equally.

Her family had standards by which they measured everyone else. In their opinion most people fell short in one way or another. There was no question in Darcy's mind as to how they would react to her being a waitress. She smiled at her imaginary picture of their exaggerated response to such news. "A waitress! What on earth can she be thinking?" Fainting spells requiring smelling salts, or a sick headache with cologne-soaked cloths applied to the forehead, would follow! Maybe she was doing them all a kindness by not telling them. Protecting them from the flood of prestige-damaging gossip that would swirl around them if the truth were known.

Besides, in a year's time she would be home, and no one would be the worse for her fiction. She might be able to turn the whole episode into a humorous story.

She mailed the letter feeling sure that her mother, aunts, and uncle would not only be glad to hear from her but also rest easy that she was safe and happy. That was the message she hoped would be passed on to Grady, to whom she had no intention of writing.

Most of the time Darcy could live her daily life as a Harvey Girl without too much pricking of her conscience. The fact that she was keeping her employment as a waitress secret from her family bothered her only occasionally. Sometimes late at night when she was falling asleep, the thought would strike and she would come wide awake. She would cringe. Being exposed as a liar was her biggest fear. The longer she let it go, the harder it became to tell the truth. However, except for those times, Darcy found it easy to make excuses, justify what she'd done. Wasn't she protecting her family from malicious or petty gossip?

All these doubts and questions came sharply into focus one day when she was taking a break between the arrivals of trainloads of passengers. Darcy was curled up on her bed, reading one of Clemmie's copies of the *Ladies' Home Gazette,* when Clemmie came into their dormitory room.

"Here's your mail. I picked it up when I got mine," she said, tossing Darcy a bunch of letters.

When she was in Topeka in training, Darcy had sent a notice to the post office in Juniper Junction to forward her mail in care of Harvey House. She had sent a similar notice to reroute her mail to Emporia. This was the first batch of mail she had received from Willowdale.

Sifting through the pile of envelopes, she recognized the different handwriting. Her mother's neat cursive, Auntie Sadie's tilted, cramped style, Aunt Maude's strong, bold strokes, and her friend Carly Hampton's curlicued back-hand. Which should she read first?

She decided she'd start with her mother's, then read Aunt Maude's, then Auntie Sadie's, and save for last Carly's, which she figured would be filled with the latest news of their crowd, along with Carly's personal opinions. Maybe about Grady?

She opened her mother's first.

My Dear Daughter,
I have thought of you every day since we put you on the train to Kansas—and to Juniper Junction, of all places. It's too late, I know, to say anything more about your foolhardy decision. I know you acted on impulse, on the spur of the moment, but I feel in my heart it was a mistake and you will live to regret it.

Poor Grady has been here almost every day to ask about you and if we have heard anything. What can I tell him? Except that we received a telegram saying you had arrived safely and that you were checking out a change of teaching posts. I do hope the new one is to your liking. I never thought of you becoming a teacher, if the truth were known. I pictured you happily married and living just down the street. We all still think Grady is a fine young man, and without holding out false hope to him, I did try to comfort him by saying that distance and absence make the heart grow fonder. As your grandmother always says, running away from a problem never solves it. You only hurt yourself and everyone else concerned.

I do pray that when your year's contract is completed, you may have changed your mind about Grady and want to set-tle down here close to your folks, where you grew up. It is my belief that happiness lies close to home, where you have

*friends and family who care about you and are concerned
about your future. Remember the sampler that your grandmother, our dear Mama, cross-stitched that hangs in the
upstairs hall? "Seek home for rest, for home is best." Do write
soon and put all my fears at ease. I pray every day for your
safety and well-being.*

Ever your devoted Mother

Darcy put her mother's letter aside with a sigh. There
was no point in upsetting her with the real facts. Her
mother had lived all her life in Willowdale, had never traveled or known any other people than her family and close
friends. She would never understand Darcy's taking such a
risk as she had!

Next she opened Aunt Maude's letter. As she read it,
she could almost hear her aunt's strident voice.

My Dear Niece,
*I do not need to tell you how dismayed we all are at your
reckless decision. It was hardly a well-considered one.*

*You and your mother have lived with us since you were
a little girl, after your father died. We opened our home to
you, and we have tried to be as parents to you, protecting,
guiding, advising. As you know, we strongly objected to your
impulsive rejection of the upstanding young man to whom
you were promised, and then your going off on your own. It
is something we cannot condone. Perhaps even now you regret
what you did and are properly remorseful. I hope so. It is my
sincere prayer that you have now seen the error of your ways
and sincerely regret all the hurt you have caused those of us
who have nurtured and cherished you all these years. We
expected more of you than this.*

And if you are under the mistaken belief that Grady is dying of a broken heart over you, let me assure you that you have another thing coming. We saw him at the political rally and barbecue just this past Saturday, and he looked fit as a fiddle, spruced up and as good-looking as you could imagine. And don't think all the girls in town didn't let him know it. He was surrounded by admiring young women all day long. The applause he got after making a short speech was especially gratifying to your Uncle Henry, who as you know gave Grady his sponsorship in running for sheriff. You would have thought he was William Jennings Bryan or the president himself. Mark my words, some enterprising young lady is going to make off with him if you don't come to your senses.

In closing, I remind you that the members of your family are not getting any younger, and in the years to come you may weep bitter tears over what you have done.

We know you have signed a contract to remain in your position for a year. But you can write a letter expressing your remorse, admit you were wrong, and apologize to all of us. Grady certainly deserves that much. That's the least you can do.

Your concerned and caring Aunt Maude

Darcy suppressed a groan. Aunt Maude certainly was an expert in pouring on the guilt, rubbing salt in the wound. She folded the thin stationery pages and replaced them in the envelope. If Aunt Maude hoped the result would be a penitent Darcy's return of a letter thick with apologies, she was wrong. In fact, it spurred Darcy's intention to write the most enthusiastic letter she could compose about her new life—of course, leaving out the basic fact that she was actually waitressing instead of teaching.

Auntie Sadie's note was typical of the childlike, sweet-natured creature she was, the exact opposite of her older sister Maude.

Oh, my darling Darcy, how we do miss you! The house seems so empty without the sounds of your laughter, your footsteps running up the stairs, your singing when you were happy—which was most of the time, until that last week and your tiff with Grady. Well, I guess it was more than a tiff, wasn't it? I wept many times recalling how I tried to get you to forgive him, not burn all your bridges behind you. But it was of no use. You wouldn't listen; your mind was made up. And I understand that. Believe me, nobody could convince me that I was wrong when I broke my engagement. Looking back long years ago, it was over as simple a thing as seeing Milford kissing Lucyanne McCall under the mistletoe at the Christmas party. But I was young and he was my first love, and we had made each other all sorts of promises, and most of all I had kissed him! And allowed him to kiss me! Many times! And in those days that was serious business, let me tell you. Anyway, I did regret it, and I wanted to save you those same feelings of wishing you had it to do over.

No matter what Maude may tell you, Grady is moping around town with a woebegone expression. I'm sure he's wishing he'd never agreed to run for sheriff, for all the attention he's getting.

If you can, try to remember, "The course of true love never runs smooth," and maybe when you've both had time enough to think about it, you might change your mind and somehow get back together when you come home to Willowdale. Oh my, a year seems so long, darling, but remember, nothing is forever. Take care and stay well and remember, your doting

Auntie Sadie keeps you in her loving thoughts and prayers always.

Darcy had to brush away a few tears after reading this. Auntie Sadie was such a dear.

Last of all she opened her friend Carly's letter with anticipation.

The first part was full of comments about social events Darcy was missing—a graduation, a square dance, and a church box supper—and what Carly had worn to these occasions. Then she began telling Darcy how she admired her for the daring adventure she had undertaken.

You always were so brave. I remember how you always took a dare. Even from the boys when we were in grammar school. Like the time you jumped off the toolshed roof, and the other time you climbed old Mr. Sander's tree to shake down apples for the rest of us, and he came out with his pitchfork, shaking his fist and yelling. You never blinked an eyelash. Just stood there, hands on your hips, sweet-talking him. I think you told him everyone said he grew the best apples in the county, ought to win first prize at the fair! You always got away with whatever you did. I guess that's what I envy about you most.

I guess you want to know what everybody in Willowdale is saying about you. It's plenty, let me tell you. The thing most of the girls say is that you were a fool to break your engagement to Grady. He is really the center of attention now. You have to admit, he's really good-looking. And lately he's been dressing up. Somebody must be buying his clothes for him at Taber's Dry Goods and Clothing Store. He's wearing Texas-style boots and a wide-brimmed Stetson hat. I hope that doesn't make you mad to hear. He doesn't look a bit down in the mouth. How could he? Someone's always clinging on his arm, looking up at him adoringly, hanging on his every word. Maybe that's what it takes to get to be sheriff? I don't know what you're feeling right now, but I still admire you for having the gumption to leave Willowdale and see the world. I can't much see you as a teacher, but there must be some social life where you are. I always read in western romances that a schoolmarm is popular and has lots of ranchers, cowboys, and such courting her. I know you'll have lots to tell me when you write. So please do write. You must have some time of your own after correcting papers and paddling kids (I'm teasing; you probably are the nicest teacher in the world). Good luck anyhow. I'll try to keep you posted on our town's doings—and the outcome of the election, for sure.

Darcy smiled as she finished Carly's letter. If her friend knew the truth, she would know that there was not much social life here. At least for Harvey Girls, since they were discouraged from socializing with restaurant customers or members of the staff.

Mostly Darcy was too busy to think much about or miss the active social life she had enjoyed in Willowdale.

No one here knew or cared about the privileged place she and her family had in Willowdale. She was accepted as one of them. It was nice not to be valued by a small town's measuring stick. She knew her friends, like Carly, would be astonished if they knew what she was doing. No amount of explaining would make them understand how well-thought-of the Harvey Girls were. For the time being, heavy as it lay on her heart, Darcy felt it was better to keep it secret.

"Good news from home?" Clemmie asked as Darcy gathered up her letters and started to put them in the drawer of her bedside table.

Darcy shrugged. "Nothing special."

"I got a letter from my mom," Clemmie said. "Mostly telling me about what the boys are doing. Makes me kinda homesick. But not very. Thinking about my chores back there makes our job here at Harvey House seem a snap." Clemmie laughed. "Mom isn't much for writing, but she sent the new copy of the *Ladies' Home Gazette*. There are some good stories in it this time. Can't wait to read the next installment of 'The Ghost of Highland Castle.'"

Both girls were avid fans of the romantic mystery serial that was published in the weekly women's magazine.

"When I finish, I'll give it to you to read," Clemmie promised and settled back against her pillows with the issue.

Much as Darcy tried to deny it, the letters from home had their effect. Her conscience pinched hard. No matter that her days were so full, from the minute she and Clemmie got up in the morning, served the first trainload of passengers, cleaned up their stations, and got ready for the next, until they dropped into bed at night, that she didn't seem to have a spare moment. Writing such a complicated letter of explanation became harder and harder.

Sometimes she lay sleepless at night, asking herself how she had ever got into this mess. Where along the way had not telling the truth become an easy habit so that keeping this big secret had seemed justifiable? All the dozens of little white lies she had told through the years came back to disturb her. Excuses for being late, forgetting an errand, not turning in homework, not accepting an invitation—all mounted up to dishonesty. A habit of fudging on the truth built up over the years. Darcy's cheeks burned in the dark of their dormitory bedroom. She felt so guilty, while in the next bed Clemmie slept the sleep of the innocent. She wanted to change; she was trying. But how to undo what she had already done?

NINE

Most of the time Darcy was too busy to give much thought to what might have been had she not left Willowdale so impulsively.

However, sometimes unwarranted thoughts about Grady floated into her mind just before she fell asleep. She still couldn't believe how he could have broken his promise. She knew him so well. Or thought she did. After all, they had grown up together. Since grammar school days, when he had been the class cutup and relentless tease. When they got to high school, he was too tall, too self-conscious and bashful to show his feelings. However, by the time he came back to Willowdale after two years at the state agricultural college, the rest of him had caught up with his height. His lean build fit his six-foot frame, his features had become strong, and his shy manner had a boyish charm that was very appealing.

It was then he earnestly started courting Darcy, with everyone's approval. Not that the course of their romance had all gone smoothly. They were both strong-willed. But more often than not their conflicts ended in laughter, not acrimony.

Darcy couldn't help remembering that year with some nostalgia. So many happy memories of things they had done together. That first summer had been filled with fun. Attending the county fair, cotton candy and carousel music, Ferris wheel rides and square dances. Church box suppers where Grady always knew which one to bid on so that together they could eat Aunt Maude's fried chicken and Auntie Sadie's caramel cake. Walks along woodland paths in autumn, holding hands, their boots crunching on the fallen leaves. In the winter, sledding down the hill behind the Sanders' barn, skating when Mallard's Pond froze over. Taffy pulls and popcorn parties. And at Christmastime, the frosty snow-filled air, going caroling with the youth choir, and kisses under the mistletoe . . .

Funny how the slightest thing could send Darcy down memory lane. A whiff of scent, a snatch of a certain melody, an arriving customer who for a minute reminded her of Grady.

It is said that a woman never forgets her first love. Grady had been hers. No matter what, she knew she would never forget him.

Everyone expected them to get married. The fact that they hadn't was, in Darcy's opinion, Grady's fault. Why had he listened to all those well-meaning folks, with their own axes to grind, urging him to run for sheriff? Maybe he thought she would come around. Well, he had been wrong.

Darcy remembered the day of their terrible quarrel vividly. She was having a last fitting of her wedding dress in Auntie Sadie's upstairs sewing room and from the window saw Grady coming across the street to the house.

"Get me out of this," Darcy urged her aunt, shaking her arms out of the sleeves. "Grady's coming. I've got to go."

"Hold on a minute, honey—you'll pull out those pins! Grady's not going anywhere. He came to see you, didn't he?" Auntie Sadie teased as she carefully held the dress so Darcy could step out of the trailing gown.

Hurriedly Darcy slipped on her blouse and fastened the waistband on her skirt and ran down the hall. She had just reached the landing at the top of the stairs when she heard Uncle Henry greeting Grady.

"Well, howdy, young fellow. So, you've thrown your hat in the ring and are in the sheriff's race? They told me at the courthouse you'd just signed your filing papers."

"Yes, sir," Grady said.

"Well, that's good. I think you'll do fine."

"Thank you, sir." Grady sounded pleased.

Overhearing this exchange, Darcy felt her heart chill. Her hand tightened on the banister rail as Uncle Henry spoke again.

"Should be a fairly easy race. Don't think you'll have any trouble—"

"Oh, no? He doesn't know what trouble is yet!" Darcy's harsh tone of voice startled even her. Both Grady and her uncle looked up at her as she came down the steps.

Darcy's heart was pumping. A pulse in her temple pounded. She stared at Grady accusingly.

"How could you? Without even talking to me. You promised. You gave me your word."

Grady shifted from one foot to the other. He looked at her uncle for support.

Taken aback by his niece's outburst, Uncle Henry began, "Now look here, young lady—"

"*You* look here, Uncle Henry. This is between me and Grady."

Uncle Henry turned red in the face. Darcy had never spoken to him that way. She was trembling. Involuntarily Henry took a few steps away.

Darcy turned back to Grady. "Knowing how I feel about being in politics, you went behind my back and—" At a loss for words at his betrayal, she halted. Grady started to say something but she cut him off. She tugged at her engagement ring and held it out to him. "Here, take this back. How can I marry someone I can't trust?"

Grady looked shaken. "Aw, honey, please. I can explain."

"There's nothing to explain. You broke your solemn promise to me. That's it." Darcy spun around and moved toward the stairs. She caught a glimpse of Aunt Maude standing frozen in the doorway of the parlor and saw the shocked faces of her mother and Auntie Sadie leaning over the balcony above. They all must have witnessed the scene.

"Wait, Darcy, please—," Grady pleaded.

Darcy shook her head and started up the steps. His voice followed her. "Darcy, we gotta talk. Honey, please."

"There's nothing to talk about. It's over."

Darcy remembered rushing up the steps, brushing by her mother and Auntie Sadie, who both held out restraining hands to her as she went past. Ignoring them, tears streaming down her cheeks, she had half run, half stumbled down the hall to her bedroom. She slammed the door and flung herself down on the bed, sobbing.

Of course, she had had to talk to Grady again. There had been endless talks, but she had remained stubborn. And so had he. It was a tug of war between them—Grady asserting his manhood right to choose his own profession, Darcy determined not to budge from her ultimatum.

In the end she had answered the ad for a teacher in Juniper Junction.

There were moments, even now, when Darcy recalled how falling in love had been. That summer she was nineteen and first noticed the grown-up Grady newly returned home from college. It was like summer lightning. Swift, sudden, stunning. She remembered the thrill of their first kiss, the first faltering words of love, the promises made . . .

That's what had done it. If he had really loved her, he wouldn't have broken his promise.

She was better off without him. He didn't deserve her loyalty. Or the truth about where she was and what she was doing. Let him wonder and worry and miss her. It served him right.

He was probably on the campaign trail now and loving every minute. And she? Well, her new life was just as different and interesting and full of unexpected rewards. Except for the troubling undercurrent that she was living a lie in relation to her family and the people in Willowdale, Darcy found she was happier than she ever thought she could be.

In spite of all the Harvey rules and regulations, Darcy was experiencing a sense of freedom as delicious as it was strange.

The Harvey system was a strict teacher. However, Darcy was learning a great deal from this experience. She was becoming more responsible, more punctual, more attentive to details, and learning to get along with all sorts of people. In the Harvey system, everyone was treated the same no matter what their job was—chefs, busboys, waitresses. All work was honorable and respected. There was no acceptable excuse not to follow directions, cooperate, be generous and helpful. It was character building, and surprisingly Darcy really liked how she was changing.

TEN

DECEMBER 1903

Although Christmas was coming and thoughts of home and family were often in Darcy's mind, it didn't seem a good time to write an explanatory letter to her family. Why spoil Christmas with news that would upset them? With her salary and generous tips, Darcy had accumulated a nice little nest egg. She spent a good part of it buying extravagant presents for each member of her family and enclosed in the package she sent home an ambiguous description of the holidays she was enjoying. She used the Harvey House special holiday menu to describe the festive meal she would be sharing with friends. That much was true. Since there weren't many travelers on

Christmas Eve or Christmas, the staff was treated to a gourmet feast of the best of the restaurant's cuisine.

> *Dear Family,*
> *I am sure you will be happy to know that Christmas is celebrated out west much as it is in Willowdale. Of course, I shall miss Auntie Sadie and Aunt Maude's sweet potato pies. But there are some marvelous cooks here too. There will be the traditional turkey, of course, all sorts of relishes and vegetables.*

Darcy did not dare put in some of the chefs' prize dishes which would also be served to show off their skills. She had some qualms of conscience as she wrote. She soon dismissed them. Who was it really hurting? She never actually lied. And who would ever know?

The fact that she herself knew was bad enough. She squirmed uncomfortably when Clemmie said her church was putting on a Christmas pageant with a special music program, and invited her to come. Going to church seemed hypocritical under the circumstances, but Darcy saw no way to avoid it.

After they had finished dinner service, cleaned their station, and set up their tables for breakfast, Clemmie and Darcy hurried back to their room to dress and leave for church.

The little church was beautifully decorated, and as Clemmie had assured her, hearing the choir sing was like listening to a band of angels. Darcy found herself remembering other Christmases when she had attended church with her family. Sometimes she had been inattentive, daydreaming perhaps of a new dress she was wearing or a holiday party she was going to the next evening. But this night everything about the service seemed especially lovely and meaningful. She was more appreciative of the true reason, more mindful of whose birthday they were celebrating.

Darcy particularly liked the simplicity of the minister's sermon.

"It is Christmas, and I wish you happiness today and for every tomorrow in the new year. It is a time to rejoice and be glad for the gift of the world's greatest life. It is time to praise God and be grateful for the daily miracles we tend to take too much for granted."

His words lingered with her after church. As she and Clemmie walked through the starlit night back to their dormitory, Darcy had to really face what she was doing, the deception about her job. With New Year's just around the corner, she made a resolution that at the first of the year she would write a full letter of explanation to her family.

However, the very next morning something unexpected happened to change the direction of her life. She and Clemmie were called into the manager's office and told that two vacancies had occurred and that they were being transferred to the restaurant at the newly established Harvey House hotel in Redsands, Arizona. They were given railroad passes and told to pack up immediately because they would be leaving the next day on the morning train.

Both girls were thrilled. What an adventure lay ahead! They had heard how beautiful Arizona was and that the Harvey House there was one of the most elegant on the whole Santa Fe line and welcomed the most glamorous guests.

That night in a frenzy of excitement Darcy packed. As she did, she came across the box containing her engagement ring, where she had stuffed it in the pocket of her valise. Why she had kept it instead of sending it back to Grady, she wasn't sure. Now that she was starting a new job in a new town, a whole new set of experiences awaited her. This seemed the time to cut the last tie that bound her. So much had happened since she broke up with Grady, left Willowdale. So much had changed for her and in her. She wondered if she had ever really been in love with him. Or had she just been in love with being in love? She certainly hadn't given much thought to the duties, the responsibilities, of marriage, the commitment to another person's welfare and happiness. For that matter, had she even understood what they were?

The only thing she had known for sure was that she didn't want to live the life Grady had chosen for himself. A sheriff's wife? No, Darcy knew that wasn't for her. She replaced the little box in her valise and went on packing. When she got to Redsands and was settled in there, she would write Grady a letter and return the ring. Mentally she worded it.

> *Dear Grady,*
> *I am returning your ring. No matter what you said about not wanting to be unengaged, it is for the best. We were not meant for each other. I hope someday you will find a girl who is more suited to the kind of life you want.*
> *With sincere good wishes . . .*

That should once and for all leave no doubt that she meant it. It might sound stiff and cold, but what else could she say? It seemed she had already said it all in the talks they'd had before she left Willowdale. Besides, a returned engagement ring would probably not cause half so much gossip as the truth she was hiding.

She would write to both her family and Grady from Arizona. She could only imagine what kind of reaction would be in the next batch of mail from Willowdale.

PART
THREE

PART
THREE

ELEVEN

As soon as Darcy and Clemmie got off the train in Arizona, they exchanged happy smiles. It was like stepping onto an entirely different planet. The sunshine, the warm breeze, the mild climate, the Indians camped at the depot, selling their wares of pottery and woven rugs and blankets, the mountains visible behind the Harvey House hotel—all seemed strange and exotic.

The hotel was built in the style of a Spanish hacienda, with stucco over adobe brick, a red tile roof, long arched porches, and a center courtyard surrounded by colorful flower beds. In the middle of the courtyard stood a circular fountain. Inside the hotel were seventy-five guest rooms, plus parlors, a barbershop, a club, a reading room, and the dining room.

Between the hotel and the train station was a two-hundred-foot arcade, like a mission cloister, leading to the museum and gift shop featuring Indian arts and crafts. Inside were rooms where tourists could watch weavers, potters, silversmiths, bead makers, and basket makers at work.

The Harvey House hotel and restaurant, with its excellent cuisine and service, its romantic atmosphere, was also the social center of the town. Civic and private events such as wedding receptions and banquets of various kinds were held here. Its attractive furnishings, with much use of the native art, rugs, pottery, drew a wide clientele. Outside the dining room, a brick patio with a fountain and abundant flowers had tables at which patrons could visit and socialize before coming inside to eat.

The Harvey House code was so well established throughout the system that Clemmie and Darcy had no trouble fitting easily into their new assignment. The same rules and regulations, the same pattern of serving, were in effect here as in all the other Harvey House restaurants.

Swept up into the excitement of her beautiful new surroundings, Darcy put off writing the letter to her family. Instead she sent a telegram with a few lines simply stating,

A new job opportunity presented itself, and I decided to take it. I will write soon.

Somehow the dramatic step of writing to Grady and returning his ring faded in importance. In the enjoyment of her new everyday life, filled with new sights, experiences, she never got around to doing it.

She sent many picture postcards of the area: colorful images of the picturesque town, its unusual architecture, the flowers, and the local Native Americans in their colorful garb. This seemed to her to offset the need for details about her job. She had read Helen Hunt Jackson's novel *Ramona* and not only had been enchanted by the romance but also had developed a sympathy for Native Americans. She was fascinated by their jewelry-making skills, their intricately designed woven rugs and blankets, and their original pottery with its unique painted motifs.

Darcy justified her lack of candor by assuring herself there was no real lie in anything she wrote. Except of course the insinuation that she was working as a teacher. She still winced, picturing the reaction of her relatives if the truth were known. It had gone on for months now, and the situation seemed too complicated. Somehow Darcy didn't know how to untangle it all.

Midwinter in Arizona brought a flock of travelers into the restaurant. The clientele was interesting. Many came from the North and East, seeking the warmth of the climate, the scenic beauty of the area, and the chance to view another way of life, as demonstrated by the Native Americans, whose traditions were the same as they had been for hundreds of years before the white man came.

Darcy loved her new assignment. Among the train passengers who came and stayed for periods of time at the adjoining hotel were some whose names were seen on theater marquees, on best-selling books, on the national political scene. Actors, artists, writers—the affluent and influential from all walks of life. These people, most of them seeking anonymity, enjoyed being unrecognized, so they could relax. Harvey Girls were taught to treat everyone the same regardless of their celebrity.

That's why the arrival of the Edistons, a U.S. senator and his wife placed at Darcy's station, was not handled as a special event.

Congress was in recess, and this was the couple's usual time to take an Arizona vacation. As she served them at every meal, Darcy learned they came every year.

Elizabeth Ediston was Darcy's idea of a lady of refinement—tall, willowy, dressed in the best of taste. Her hair, always beautifully coifed, was a silvery blond, her features aristocratic. Her manner was reserved. She spoke in a low voice, never asked for any special service, and always left a generous tip.

Roger Ediston was the total opposite. He was gregarious and outgoing. In appearance he looked just like a senator should, portly with flowing silver hair and a well-trimmed mustache. He was openly cordial, had a smile for everyone, staff and fellow hotel guests alike. Upon entering the dining room, he would stop at various tables, seeming to recognize people, to shake hands or give someone a pat on the shoulder. In a way he reminded Darcy of her uncle, who always seemed to be running for election. However, the rumor circulating through the hotel was that this would be Senator Ediston's last term in office.

It seems the real reason for their frequent trips to Arizona was Mrs. Ediston's frail health. This was confirmed to Darcy by Mrs. Ediston herself. The day before they were to return to Washington, D.C., she confided, "I shall miss it here, Darcy. How I dread leaving. It's so peaceful and relaxing here, compared with all the frenzy of life in the capital."

"We'll be sorry to see you go, Mrs. Ediston."

"Thank you, Darcy. You have made our mealtimes here especially pleasant. You're such a lovely young lady. I'm sure your family must be very proud of you."

Darcy felt a clutch of guilt. *Proud of me? Not if they knew the truth! Or what a liar I am!*

Mrs. Ediston continued as she sipped her tea, "The only thing that makes leaving bearable is that we will be back in the spring and eventually will be coming back to stay. We fell in love with Arizona on our first trip here, and both of us decided it would be the perfect place to retire. We had a Washington architect draw up plans for us to build a permanent home here. The architect will scout the area and select a site. When we come in the spring, we'll make the decision." Darcy saw Mrs. Ediston's excited anticipation in her eyes and heard it in her voice. "While the house is under construction, we'll be staying here as usual. So this isn't good-bye, Darcy."

"That's good news. I'm so glad to hear that, Mrs. Ediston."

When the Edistons departed on the noon train the next day, Darcy felt better knowing they would be returning.

Another Harvey House guest arrived the following day and was assigned to Darcy's station. A direct contrast to Elizabeth Ediston, she was stocky and of indeterminate age. Her dark, wispy hair was worn in a careless bun and was threaded with silver streaks; her face was lined, sun-coarsened, probably by an active outdoor life. She rode horseback every morning. She came into the dining room in her riding outfit of jodhpurs and denim jacket and ordered a hearty breakfast. The first day Darcy waited on her, she speared Darcy with a penetrating look, then announced, "I'm Clara Bingham," as if Darcy should recognize the name. Trained that all customers of the restaurant were to be treated the same no matter who they were, Darcy showed no particular awe. The woman asked, "You're new, aren't you?"

Darcy smiled and answered that she was.

The next question was, "How do you like being a waitress? I should think a young woman as pretty and presumably smart as you would find a better job than waitressing."

Darcy was indignant at this assertion. She drew herself up proudly. "I'm a Harvey Girl; that's different."

"No need to get huffy." Clara seemed amused. "I'm sure it must have benefits I don't know about. What would you say they were?" She eyed Darcy curiously.

Darcy did not answer but went on serving her, refilling her coffee cup several times. She did not initiate any more conversation. Neither did Clara Bingham.

After Miss Bingham left the dining room, Darcy realized she had actually been offended by the woman's remark about being a waitress. She was proud of being a Harvey Girl. Now that she knew what it took to be one, she was very proud indeed.

Later when she and Clemmie were in their room taking their break between train arrivals, Darcy was glancing through her roommate's new copy of the *Ladies' Home Gazette.* Suddenly she let out a gasp and sat straight up. "Will you look at this!" She thumped a page of the magazine with her index finger. "Japan! She's been to Japan! Lived there. This is all about her travels there!"

"What, what? Will I look at what?"

"Clara Bingham. *My* Clara Bingham. Right here in the *Gazette!*" Darcy held up the magazine, pointing to the lead article. "She's a famous writer and she's sitting at my station."

Clemmie seemed unimpressed. "So? Lots of famous people come to Harvey House."

"Maybe. But I've got one sitting right at my table three times a day. Well, almost three times. Breakfast and dinner, anyway."

Intrigued by her new customer, Darcy determined to get to know Clara Bingham better. She bent the rules a little by asking her questions while serving her. The journalist was quite willing to share some of her adventures.

At each meal Clara told Darcy a little more about herself. And Darcy was impressed. Clara wrote for a large publishing chain consisting of magazines and newspapers, including some of the best-known periodicals in the country. She had been almost everywhere. Africa, India, the Himalayas, traveling alone, under hazardous conditions, sometimes in dangerous situations. Darcy had never known anyone like her. A single, independent woman with a career. Clara was intelligent, funny, and articulate. She was clever, quick, and interested in everything.

What Darcy did not discover at the time was that on this trip, Clara was riding the entire railroad system through the Southwest, doing research for a series of travel articles featuring various places along the way. Arizona was her current area of concentration.

As the days went on, the two became friends. Darcy enjoyed waiting on Clara, hearing about her adventures, and little by little the journalist drew Darcy out about her life as a Harvey Girl.

Harvey Girls were not encouraged to enter into personal conversations with the people they served, but it seemed to Darcy that this rule hardly applied to the friendship she and Clara had developed.

One morning at breakfast Clara remarked, "People come to Arizona for different things. The reason most give when asked is that they came to find the 'good life.' I think that more often it's to find themselves. What about you, Darcy? What did you come to Arizona for?"

"Maybe to find myself," Darcy answered lightly as she filled Clara's coffee cup.

Clara gave her a sharp look. "Really? Come now, how can a smart young woman like you find yourself waiting tables?"

"Well then, happenstance!" Darcy laughed. "A chance meeting on a train? Does that suit you better?"

"That sounds like a good story." Clara's sharp eyes brightened as she looked at Darcy over the rim of her cup.

"Oh, it is. You can add a broken engagement to that to make it even better."

"Go on, I'm all ears." Clara set her cup down and leaned forward.

"Better still," Darcy said, smiling mischievously, "my job is a well-kept secret." She lowered her voice. "I'm supposed to be teaching school. My family would have a fit if they knew I was working as a waitress." She paused. "But I love it. I've never been happier. Being a Harvey Girl is the best."

"I congratulate you." Clara nodded her approval. "I admire a young woman with spunk. It's important to be your own person."

Darcy certainly did admire Clara Bingham. She had never met anyone like her. Certainly not in Willowdale, where a single woman past the age of twenty-five was called an old maid and was looked upon with pity if not scorn.

Getting to know Clara Bingham gave Darcy a new perspective. Maybe it was possible for a woman to chart her own course in life, not conform to the traditional roles women were expected to take. Even among the Harvey staff were examples of women who had done just that. Viola Colby, the personnel manager in Topeka, for one; Paula Casey, the head waitress in Emporia. Both led independent lives. They dressed stylishly on their days off, took advantage of the policy of free railroad passes for employees. Paula Casey had even gone to California on her last vacation. Darcy began to think of what her future might be within the benevolent Harvey system. A chance to see the world, explore the possibilities of travel. The future seemed wider, less limited, than it had only months ago.

TWELVE

Darcy loved everything about Arizona. She enjoyed the mild climate, the extraordinary beauty of the area, the outdoor life it offered. On their days off, she and Clemmie went hiking and sometimes rented horses to ride into the desert. The longer she was here, the more she could imagine living in Arizona forever.

Being a Harvey Girl had broadened her horizons in every way. She was daily coming into contact with interesting people. The hotel guests were sophisticated travelers from cosmopolitan backgrounds. She was learning so much just observing them. Even though the Harvey system prohibited socializing with customers, it was natural to form warm relationships with those one served regularly. Most of the Harvey Girls received social invitations from customers not aware of the rules, Darcy had not found this Harvey code hard to live by. That is, until one morning when a tall young man walked into the restaurant.

Darcy was on the breakfast shift and noticed him at once. Who wouldn't have? At six foot three he was a towering presence. At the door he removed his wide-brimmed cowboy hat and surveyed the room, then moved with a kind of athletic grace over to the counter and sat down.

In spite of his cowboy appearance, he spoke with an eastern accent as he ordered one of Harvey's famous cinnamon rolls—always served warm from the oven—and coffee, black.

As she poured his coffee, Darcy had a chance to observe him at close range. His features were strongly molded in a deeply tanned face, his eyes very blue. He wore a blue shirt under a riding jacket of worn tweed with leather elbow patches. He thanked her courteously as she placed his plate before him.

Soon after that first morning, Darcy could almost set her watch by him. Every day as soon as the restaurant opened, he arrived in a fresh shirt, cleanly shaved, his hair combed neatly. For breakfast he always sat at the counter, acknowledging Darcy with a shy smile and a cheerful "Good morning."

In the evenings he dined in the restaurant alone at a table in Darcy's station. He was very polite, speaking in a cultured voice and always leaving a large tip.

None of this was lost on Clemmie. She began to tease Darcy about him. "I think he's sweet on you."

At first Darcy dismissed that claim. But after two weeks she could not deny it. It was too obvious. She could feel his eyes upon her as she went about her regular duties in the dining room, setting up tables in her station, placing the plates just so, lining up the flatware, arranging the cups and saucers, folding the napkins. The fact that it did not annoy her was surprising. He was always perfectly gentlemanly when he addressed her. It was Clemmie who learned his name from the hotel desk clerk and informed Darcy.

"His name is Ted Shepherd. He's not a cowboy or a cattleman. He's from back east. From Maryland, it says on the hotel register."

"Leave it to you, Clemmie. Did you ever consider becoming a Pinkerton detective?" Darcy said, rolling her eyes and pretending not to be too interested.

"Want to know what else I found out?"

Darcy shrugged with pretended indifference.

"Well, all right, then—" Clemmie turned away.

"Wait! Yes, sure I want to know," Darcy admitted.

"I also found out he rents a horse and rides out to the desert every morning before he comes in here for breakfast. He may be looking for ranch property. Could be he's looking to settle down here. Maybe looking for a wife?"

"More likely he plans to bring a bride out here when he finds what he wants," suggested Darcy, hoping it wasn't so.

"More important, when is he ever going to get up enough nerve to say more to you than 'Good morning' or

'Good evening' or 'Much obliged' or 'Thank you, miss' when he's finished?" demanded Clemmie.

"What good would that do?" countered Darcy. "Remember, he's a hotel guest as well as a restaurant customer."

However, Darcy considered the possibilities. Maybe on her next free day she could rent a horse herself and ride out to the desert. No one could say anything if she happened to meet Ted Shepherd on the trail and had a friendly conversation, could they?

Before Darcy could act upon her vague idea, something unexpected happened.

One evening when Ted had finished his meal, Darcy came forward to clear his table. Instead of thanking her, placing the tip under his plate, and leaving, as he usually did, he remained seated. She continued removing the silver and plates onto her tray, trying not to be aware that he seemed to be deliberately lingering.

Finally he got to his feet, took a few steps, then turned back. "By the way, miss, I just wondered—do you ride? I mean, if you do, would you like to go riding sometime? With me?"

Startled, Darcy stared at him. Had he been reading her mind? She felt a rush of pleasure. Clemmie was right. He was interested in her. She hesitated. Wouldn't it be all right to go horseback riding? Then her better judgment took over. What if someone saw them and reported back to the manager? Why risk getting fired? The idea of sneaking around to be with a man who was essentially still a stranger, the notion of carrying on a clandestine association, didn't appeal to her. She was finding her ongoing deception to be a wearying burden. Why take on more guilt?

Darcy darted a quick look over her shoulder to where the head waitress, Miss Cannon, was standing, then said in a low voice, "I'm sorry, I can't. I mean, we aren't supposed to...you know...go out with hotel guests."

Ted looked genuinely disappointed. After a minute's pause he said, "I understand. Sorry. Actually, I'm leaving to go back east day after tomorrow. I just thought it might be possible—" He halted as if not sure how to go on.

Darcy saw Miss Cannon looking at her curiously. Probably wondering about her prolonged conversation with one of the male diners. Darcy's station was still not completely cleared, nor had the tablecloth been removed.

"I have to go," Darcy murmured. She quickly gathered the rest of the dishes onto her tray.

She was sorry to see Ted Shepherd leave. She wished it had been possible to get to know him. She felt as if somehow she'd missed something. Something important.

She did miss seeing him every day. More than she could have guessed. She missed seeing him come in the dining room door and look around for her. She also missed the silly little flutter she got at the sight of him. His shy smile and the way his blue eyes seemed to light up when he saw her. *How foolish!* she chided herself. She hardly knew him.

Even so, she had been attracted to Ted Shepherd more than she liked to admit, more than she was willing to confess, even to Clemmie. The fact that she might never see him again made her strangely sad.

She compared her feelings about him with how she had once felt about Grady. Actually, she couldn't remember what that had been like.

THIRTEEN

After Ted Shepherd left, life at Harvey House for Darcy settled down to routine again. Not that she didn't still enjoy her job; there just wasn't that little expectant spark that had existed with his coming and going.

However, as she continued to improve as a waitress and the work became increasingly automatic, she had more time to think. The lie she was living still nagged her. The longer it went on, the harder and harder it would be to explain it. Most of the time she tried not to think about it.

Back east people had a distorted picture of the West, drawn from the sensational tabloids and the popular, exaggerated "Wild West" stories, with all their lurid details about barroom brawls and shoot-outs, about Billy the Kid, the

James Brothers, and other outlaws. In fact, a common saying was, "West of Dodge City there is no Sunday. West of Tombstone there is no God." This of course was totally untrue. There were several churches in Redsands. Clemmie had found a church she liked and attended regularly. One Sunday Clemmie persuaded Darcy to come with her.

"There's going to be a special speaker tonight, an evangelist with a powerful message. He's really good. I heard him once in a tent meeting back home."

Darcy felt a prick of conscience. In Willowdale she had always attended church with her family because it was expected of her. Often bored, inattentive, nonetheless she felt the guilt of a sinner without knowing the joy of the saint. It was her own fault. She had always resisted when an altar call was given, too embarrassed to go up in front of all those people. Besides, everyone in the Willowdale church had probably assumed she was already saved.

But Darcy could not come up with any reason to turn down Clemmie's invitation. On second thought, it would be a good thing to mention in one of her letters home that she had attended this revival and heard this preacher. With some inner reluctance she agreed to accompany Clemmie to church.

The choir was already singing when they entered the church. They found places and had just settled into the pew when two men came in from the side entrance and took seats in the chairs at the front. After the choir finished their hymn and filed out, one of the men came to the podium and announced, "Since Brother Barry has an important message to deliver tonight, I won't take up any of his time." He turned and gestured to the man who had accompanied him into the church.

Brother Barry, a robust fellow with a wiry mane of rusty gray hair, rose, came to the podium, and thumped down the tattered Bible he was carrying. In a voice that resonated to the back of the building, he greeted everyone. "Well, praise the Lord, folks, it's good to be with you tonight. And don't think any of you is here tonight by chance. You're here by divine appointment, and this message is for you."

Darcy squirmed a little uncomfortably as Clemmie gave her a knowing look. For some reason, nerves most likely, Darcy felt an irrepressible urge to giggle.

She dug her fingernails into her palms. She had a history of laughing at the wrong times, in the wrong places. As a child she had been banished from Sunday school a number of times for just such behavior.

She tried to concentrate on the beflowered hat of a stout woman sitting in the pew in front of them and wondered vaguely if she should retrim her own straw hat. But Brother Barry's loud, persistent voice soon penetrated Darcy's distraction.

Did Brother Barry know she would be here tonight? He seemed to be speaking directly to her.

"Today I am going to speak on what is an abomination to God according to Proverbs 12:22: 'Lying lips are an abomination to the Lord.'"

Darcy felt a prickling along her scalp, a sick, queasy feeling in her stomach. Brother Barry was right. Her being here tonight was no accident. Everything he was saying laid bare her soul. How could she ever have justified the lie she was living? The preacher's voice zoomed out to her again, striking her inmost being.

"We should not ignore the fate of Ananias and Sapphira when they lied." The preacher extended his arm, pointing his index finger. His voice deepened dramatically. "'Do not be deceived; God is not mocked. For whatever a man sows, he will also reap.' No one who knowingly lies escapes the wrath of God."

Darcy felt hot, then cold. She clenched her hands together compulsively. Waves of cold shivers swept over her. This must be what they called "conviction of sin." She had no excuses. All she could do was beg forgiveness.

"God is a just God," the preacher continued, "but he is also a merciful God. All he asks us to do is say we're sorry, and he is quick to forgive. To wipe the slate clean, to let us start over." Brother Barry stopped. For a full minute, it seemed, the congregation held its collective breath. Then the preacher asked, "Is there anyone here today who has a contrite heart, a broken spirit? Jesus can heal that. Come to the altar and let us pray for you. No one should leave here tonight with any burden on their conscience. If lying has been a problem with you and you want to repent of that sin in your life and start a new life free of guilt, shame, and lies, come now. Don't wait to reform yourself. We aren't able to do that. We can't do that. For that we need Jesus."

In a sudden flash of memory, Darcy recalled the day she had boarded the train for Kansas and found the tract that someone had left on the seat. The one that she had carelessly picked up and tossed into her handbag, the one that had claimed in bold print, "You need Jesus."

All at once she realized that was a message for her. One she had ignored. Without him she had got herself entangled in her stupid lie. She was stricken with remorse.

Brother Barry's voice went on, soothing, cajoling, compelling.

"And he already did that for us on the cross. He's more than willing to do that for you now. Just come. . . ."

The organ began playing softly. A deep longing filled her, tears stung, and she knew she had to go forward. To be free from all that guilt she'd carried all this time, the burden that had robbed her of complete joy and peace.

But she couldn't move. All around her, other people were getting up, moving down the aisle to the altar rail. Darcy debated. Did she really have to go forward in front of all these strangers? Couldn't she just repent right where she was? Ask God to forgive her? Write those letters home, whatever the price she would have to pay for lying? She was sorry. Wasn't that enough?

Her palms were slippery with perspiration. Her heart was pounding so loud, Darcy marveled that Clemmie and the man sitting on the other side of her couldn't hear it.

Clemmie nudged her with her elbow. "You all right? You look awfully pale. Are you sick?"

Darcy turned to face her. She started to speak but nothing came out. She swallowed. Should she nod yes and slip out of the pew, leave the church before she made a complete fool of herself?

Then Brother Barry's words repeated themselves in her ears: *"Don't think any of you is here tonight by chance. You're here by divine appointment, and this message is for you."*

Those words struck her very soul. This was her chance to be free of all the accumulated guilt she had tried to deny for so long. If she didn't do it now, there might not be another chance.

Almost without being aware of what she was doing, Darcy got up. She moved past Clemmie and found herself in the aisle making her way toward the altar. When she reached it, she went to her knees, burying her face in her hands. Brother Barry was saying, "Just repeat after me this simple prayer: Dear Lord, forgive me my sins. I want to make a fresh start in my life. Please help me. In Jesus' name I ask."

❦

In a daze Darcy walked back to their dormitory. Clemmie was full of questions but Darcy was unusually quiet.

"Didn't I tell you Brother Barry was great? I'd have answered the altar call myself if I hadn't been saved since I was ten years old. I thought you were, too, Darcy."

Not if you knew what a liar I was, Darcy said to herself. But she wasn't ready just yet to confess to her roommate about her long deception. She'd asked forgiveness from God and was convinced she'd received it. That was all she could handle for tonight.

What she was sure of was that something real had happened to her. Something that would change her life. She had experienced God's grace, his unmerited favor, at work in her heart.

Now she had her own work to do. First she would have to write home and tell her family everything, no matter what. Whatever happened as a result of telling them she lied, she'd accept. The Lord might have forgiven her, but her family was a different story altogether.

Clemmie finally broke the silence that had fallen between them on the way home. "Are you glad you came tonight?"

"Yes," was all Darcy managed to say. Her heart was too full of thanksgiving. The Lord had done a marvelous thing. The rest was up to her. That was the hard part. Darcy had always wanted to look good in the eyes of other people. Branding herself a liar wasn't something she looked forward to, but it had to be done.

FOURTEEN

APRIL 1904

For the next few weeks Darcy seemed to float in a cloud of euphoria. Clemmie kept giving her strange looks and finally one day demanded, "When are you going to stop being so angelic? I can't stand it. It's not like you at all. It's all very well and good that you got saved. I'm pleased about that. But I miss my old roomie, the one who teased and joked and laughed and told funny stories." She pouted. "Did you ever hear about people who were so heavenly minded, they were no earthly good?"

Darcy stared at her friend. She didn't know what to say. Here she had been trying so hard to be good, to control her little bouts of impatience or temper, and now Clemmie was criticizing her.

Clemmie rushed on. "I just want you to be natural again. Nobody expects you to be a saint. Especially not me."

"I'm sorry—," Darcy started to say. She halted for a moment, then burst out laughing. "I thought that's the way I was supposed to act after I got saved!"

Clemmie looked at her in astonishment as Darcy continued laughing. Then a slow smile overtook Clemmie's startled expression.

"Well, thank goodness. I'm glad to see that underneath all that piety, the real Darcy Welburne is there after all! I was beginning to think I'd better mend my own ways, rooming with an angel!"

Both girls laughed. However, this little exchange gave Darcy pause. Saved or not, she had not been honest with Clemmie. Clemmie didn't know the real Darcy. She had never told her about keeping her job as a Harvey Girl secret from her family. She was afraid it might hurt Clemmie to find out they would look down on an occupation Clemmie was proud of, considered to be the best thing that had ever happened to her. Also, she was afraid that Clemmie, who was the soul of honesty, would despise her for lying. To clear her conscience, she had to confess. This was as good a time as any.

"Clemmie, there's something about me you ought to know. Something I've been meaning to tell you."

Clemmie consulted her pendant watch pinned under her apron bib. "Can it wait? We'd better get down to the dining room. It's only a half hour until the next train."

So the opportunity to tell Clemmie passed. Darcy let it pass. She felt some relief. Maybe it could wait. Was there really any need to tell her? Clemmie would never meet her family. So Darcy decided not to bring it up again. It was a wrong decision, one she would regret.

That night the Edistons arrived on the evening train and came into the restaurant for dinner. Darcy thought Mrs. Ediston looked tired. She seemed drawn and pale. Her pallor accentuated her fragility. But she greeted Darcy warmly.

"It's so wonderful to be back and to see you, Darcy. Washington seems to be getting an early start on summer. The weather has been miserable, hot and humid."

The following day Mrs. Ediston came alone into the dining room and sat at Darcy's station. She looked more rested and seemed to have lost the weariness of the night before. She also was animated as she confided, "The senator's gone out to our land. He's meeting with our architect, who arrived this morning, and went to see the site he's selected for our house."

"That's wonderful. I'm so happy for you," Darcy said. The new house and the prospect that her hectic social life in Washington would soon be over, and that she could settle down here in the place she loved, had obviously given Mrs. Ediston a new lease on life.

However, there was something else on Mrs. Ediston's mind that day, and she was quick to share it with Darcy.

"Darcy, we don't want to put any pressure on you or ask a favor you wouldn't want to refuse, but the senator and

I have been discussing this since the last time we were here, when we got to know you. It seems such a good idea that I'll just ask if you'd be interested. All you can do is say no." Mrs. Ediston smiled but her eyes were anxious.

"Of course, Mrs. Ediston, you know I'd be happy to do anything for you."

Mrs. Ediston held up a graceful hand. "Wait until you hear what it is before you agree." She paused. "The senator has to return to Washington. But we've decided that it would be best for me to remain here so I could consult with our architect and supervise the work and make some of the decisions as our house is being built. However, Roger believes I need someone, a companion." She paused again. "We were thinking of you, Darcy. I know you enjoy your work here at the Harvey House, but we thought perhaps you could take a leave of absence—say for four or six months—and be my companion? It would be an ideal arrangement for me, and the senator assures me you will be well compensated. So what do you think, Darcy? Would you be too bored being an old lady's companion, her helper?"

"You're not an old lady, Mrs. Ediston!" Darcy declared indignantly. "And I'm flattered that you would want me. I just don't know. . ."

"Well, think about it. Pray about it. If it seems the right thing to do, we would be so happy." Mrs. Ediston spotted her husband entering the restaurant. "Here comes Roger."

The senator came over to the table. "Someone will be joining us," he announced. Then, inclining his head toward

Darcy, he asked his wife, "Have you spoken to Miss Welburne yet?"

"Yes. She's going to think about it."

"There's someone you should meet," the senator said to Darcy. "If you become Mrs. Ediston's companion, you'll be seeing a lot of him. The architect who is designing our house." The senator looked over Darcy's shoulder to the entrance of the restaurant. "Here he is now."

Darcy turned and to her amazement saw Ted Shepherd approaching their table.

FIFTEEN

At first Darcy was too startled to react. Ted was smiling that slow, shy smile of his as Mrs. Ediston said, "Darcy, may I introduce Ted Shepherd, our brilliant architect. Ted, this is my friend and hopefully my companion, Darcy Welburne."

All Darcy could think was, *What an amazing coincidence.* Another one in her life that seemed filled with such unexpected happenstances. Mrs. Ediston looked from one to the other, then with a knowing smile said, "Why is it I have the feeling no introduction is needed? Do you two happen to know one another?"

"Well, we've never been formally introduced," Ted's blue eyes were amused. "But thank you for making it official."

"I've waited on Mr. Shepherd when he was here before," Darcy explained.

Ted sat down in the chair the senator indicated, and was immediately engaged in conversation by him. Darcy busied herself pouring coffee all around. She couldn't wait to share this surprising turn of events with Clemmie. They had sometimes wondered if Ted Shepherd would ever come back to the Redsands Harvey House.

Darcy took their order and attended the other tables in her station. When the Edistons got up to leave, Ted excused himself and came over to speak to her. Mrs. Ediston smiled and gave a little wave as she and her husband left the dining room.

"Are you really considering becoming Mrs. Ediston's companion?" he asked.

She shrugged. "I'm not sure. I would have to get a special leave of absence. I wouldn't want to just give up my job here."

"I hope you can work it out. The senator confided in me that he is concerned about Mrs. Ediston's health. Washington summers are wicked. But he doesn't want to leave her here alone." He paused. "They think the world of you. I know the senator would be mightily relieved if you accepted."

"It's good of you to be concerned about Mrs. Ediston," Darcy murmured.

Ted looked a bit sheepish. "Truthfully, that wasn't my only concern. I was thinking that if you do decide to take the position, there'd be no restriction on us seeing each other. We could take that horseback ride into the desert."

Darcy's heart gave a little thump. "Yes, I guess we could."

"I'll be eager to know what you decide," he said, smiling.

She watched him leave, following his tall figure as he walked out of the dining room and into the lobby.

As she finished up her chores, straightened up her station, set up the tables for the next train arrival, Darcy thought about the Edistons' offer.

Would the management give her a leave of absence? The summer months were not as busy at the Arizona Harvey House, so the workload for waitresses was lighter. From June to September there were less travelers coming to the hotel and restaurant. Most people found the temperature, although dry desert heat, too hot for comfort. For the most part that left only the local restaurant clientele. The Edistons' offer interested her, especially after Ted Shepherd had made it so personal. She knew the management gave many of the girls time off. Especially those from farm families, who went home to help at planting and harvest times. This of course was different. Still, the Edistons were honored guests, and the management might make an exception in this case. All Darcy could do was ask and see what happened.

In any case, she didn't want to jeopardize her job. That thought wouldn't have crossed her mind less than a year ago. But now she was so thoroughly a Harvey Girl, that was her priority.

Mrs. Ediston had suggested that Darcy think and pray about it. Well, she'd taken half of her advice, anyway. She still felt a little guilty about praying, but she was trying to get over it.

Until she knew if she could get permission to accept, she decided not to mention it to Clemmie. After all, they'd promised to stick together on anything relating to their jobs, such as requesting to be transferred to the same location. If she became Mrs. Ediston's companion, would Clemmie feel Darcy was deserting her? Best to talk to the head waitress first, then tell Clemmie. But this was another mistake.

Eager to share with Clemmie the news about Ted Shepherd's return, she burst into their room. Clemmie was sitting on her bed reading the *Ladies' Home Gazette*. Before Darcy could say anything, Clemmie gave Darcy a furious look and, shaking the magazine at her, demanded, "So that's what you think of being a Harvey Girl?"

Puzzled, Darcy asked, "What do you mean? I don't know what you're talking about. Why are you so angry?"

Clemmie held the issue up so that Darcy could see the headline. In bold black letters across the top of the page marched the words "Harvey Girls Tame the Wild, Wild West."

For a split second Darcy stared at it. Then she saw the byline: Clara Bingham. It all came racing back to her in a flood. Of course. All the bantering conversations, the laughter. All in good fun. Darcy had never thought much about it. The journalist had enjoyed hearing about some of the mishaps, the inside jokes, the behind-the-scenes near-disasters at the restaurant. Thinking back, Darcy remembered she had babbled about all sorts of things as she served Clara Bingham her meals. Not a good idea, as it turned out. Harvey Girls were not supposed to engage in personal conversations with the diners. She had breached one of the rules of proper interaction with customers.

"Is it so awful?" Darcy sounded defensive but worried. "What does it say that's so terrible?"

"Here, read it yourself." Clemmie thrust her copy of the magazine at Darcy, then stormed out of the room.

Darcy's knees felt weak, and she sat down on the edge of her bed and started to read the article. On the whole it was a complimentary piece, with positive comments about the food, the atmosphere, the service, the attractive waitresses. There were only a few paragraphs Darcy wished Clara had not written. Although they were not attributed directly to her, Darcy recognized her own words. She searched for the ones to which Clemmie could have taken exception.

> *My regular server, a pretty girl of evident intelligence and refinement, confided that her family back east did not know she was working as a waitress. She told me, "They would have a fit, feeling as they do that a waitress is on a lower social rung. But some of the others feel it's better than being a housemaid or laundress or working in a factory."*

Darcy shook her head. She wished she had bitten her tongue before saying any of this. No wonder Clemmie's feelings were hurt. But what was done was done. What could she do to make amends?

❧

Nothing, as it turned out. The more she tried to smooth things over, the angrier Clemmie got.

"Please let me explain," Darcy began when Clemmie returned to their room to dress for the evening dinner duty.

"What's to explain?" Clemmie retorted. "It's all there in black and white. You're ashamed to tell your folks you're a Harvey Girl. Ashamed! How do you think that makes me feel?"

"But Clemmie, you don't understand . . ."

"Oh, I guess I'm too stupid."

"Of course not. I didn't mean—"

"Save your excuses, Darcy. I don't need them. And I'm not sure I'd believe them anyway. Anyone who would lie to her own family!" Her indignation seemed to leave Clemmie at a loss for anything further to add. She grabbed up her clean apron and flounced out the door, letting it bang behind her.

Darcy was devastated. She'd done a foolish thing and hurt the best friend she'd ever had. How could she make things right between them again?

She tried. After they finished their shift and came back to the dormitory, Darcy made another attempt.

Clemmie proceeded to get ready for bed, maintaining a stony silence.

"If you'd just give me a chance to tell you how it hap-pened, Clemmie," Darcy pleaded. "I never dreamed Clara Bingham would use any of the things I told her. It was just so—" Darcy searched for the right word while Clemmie went on buttoning her nightgown, folding back her bed-covers.

"I don't want to hear your feeble excuses. It's as plain as the paper it's written on," Clemmie said, getting into bed.

Darcy went over to her. "Please listen, Clemmie."

"No, I don't want to hear anything." She turned over and with her back to Darcy pulled her pillow over her head.

Darcy sighed deeply. Feeling terrible, she went back to her side of the room. She had often had tiffs with girlfriends in Willowdale. She and Carly had sometimes not spoken to each other for a couple of days over some minor disagree-ment. But it didn't last long. They soon made up and the friendship continued as before. She hoped Clemmie would get over it. It wasn't like her to hold a grudge. But in her heart Darcy knew this wasn't an ordinary argument. Clemmie felt deeply and personally injured by what Clara Bingham had written—sadly enough, in an article based a great deal on what Darcy had fed her about life as a Harvey Girl.

SIXTEEN

For the next few days Clemmie rebuffed all attempts at apologies. Darcy was miserable. More and more she was beginning to think that taking the job with Mrs. Ediston would be an escape.

As Clemmie's painful coldness continued, Darcy's anger at Clara Bingham deepened. She felt betrayed and was determined to confront her upon her return to Arizona. The journalist was on a trip through the Grand Canyon, riding a wooden dory down the Colorado River. However, she was scheduled to come back to Redsands afterward. Darcy checked with the hotel registry and found that she had reservations for the next week.

The day of her expected arrival, Darcy was tense with anticipation. From her post in the dining room she could see into the lobby. All during the luncheon service Darcy kept an eye on the reception desk. When she saw Clara Bingham check in, Darcy felt a renewed rush of indignation.

She had to wait until the luncheon customers had finished and her table was cleared, her station put in perfect order. Then, throwing caution to the wind, Darcy marched out to the patio where Clara was sitting in the sunshine. Busily writing on a notepad, the journalist was not aware of Darcy's approach until a shadow fell across her lap. Pen still in hand, Clara looked up.

"Well, hello, Darcy—," she began.

But before she could finish, Darcy blurted, "How could you?"

"How could I what?" Clara seemed genuinely puzzled.

Darcy whipped out the issue of the *Ladies' Home Gazette* she had folded and placed in her apron pocket, and she held it up. "This! I thought you were just showing a friendly interest. I didn't think you would write about it!"

Clara looked surprised. "Why not? You were delighted to tell me how much you enjoyed being a Harvey Girl. I just wrote down what you told me. Is there anything untrue in that article?"

"No, but I didn't expect to see what I'd said in print. All that personal stuff . . ."

"Reporters report. It was a very good story. I made you famous. I don't know what you're complaining about."

"But . . . but . . . ," Darcy sputtered, then halted. Suddenly all the things she had rehearsed to say seemed without foundation. Clara was right. She hadn't been forced to tell her anything. It had all just tumbled out. About Grady and the teaching job that had fallen through and how her family might feel.

Still, she made one last try. "Didn't it ever occur to you that my mother and aunts might read the *Ladies' Home Gazette*? That they might read about the Harvey Girl who was supposed to be teaching school but was actually waiting tables, and put two and two together and figure out it was me?"

Clara gave Darcy an unflinching look, then said, "Well, Darcy, that's your problem, isn't it?"

The truth of Clara's question stopped Darcy cold. Deflated, she turned and retraced her steps. She had no right to blame Clara. The writer may have taken advantage of her naïveté, but she herself was the one who had given her the material.

She also realized it was her own fault about how Clemmie had reacted and what would follow if her mother and aunts, whom she knew subscribed to the *Ladies' Home Gazette,* read the article and identified her. She had brought all this upon herself. Her stupid letters, her own lack of honesty, her procrastination—all of this was coming back to haunt her.

Her anger against Clara Bingham drained, leaving her limp. Out of sight, Darcy leaned against the patio post, drew a long, shaky breath.

Next she would have to try again to make up with Clemmie. Whatever she had to do, she was determined to get this awful thing settled between them.

Darcy rushed up the stairs to their dormitory room. When she opened the door, she saw that Clemmie had changed out of her uniform and into a traveling suit and was packing her suitcase.

Stunned, Darcy demanded, "What are you doing?"

"What does it look like?" retorted Clemmie. "I'm packing. I've taken an assignment in Albuquerque."

"You've *what?*"

"You heard me. I'm transferring to the Harvey House there." Clemmie folded two blouses and patted them down, then closed the lid of her suitcase, buckled the strap on top, and snapped the locks.

"You were going without even telling me?" Darcy's throat thickened with distress. "We always said we'd go together when we left here."

Clemmie gave her a cold stare. "I wouldn't think you'd want to be associated anymore with someone who thinks being a Harvey Girl is just a little bit better than being a laundress or a housemaid." Clemmie's usually mild voice was tinged with sarcasm.

"Oh, Clemmie, you know I didn't mean that. I was just saying—"

"Saying exactly what you must think down deep. I don't think we have anything in common anymore," Clemmie said icily. She picked up her hat, grabbed the handle of her suitcase, and started toward the door. "I've got to go. I'm taking the afternoon train."

"Wait, please, Clemmie. I'm so sorry. You're the best friend I've ever had. Can't we make up?"

A TANGLED WEB

Clemmie stood at the door, one hand on the door-knob.

"You can't unscramble eggs, Darcy. You can't take back what's been said." With that she went out the door and closed it firmly behind her.

Darcy made a futile gesture to go after her. "Please, Clemmie, forgive me!" But her voice echoed hollowly as the door clicked shut, and she heard the sound of footsteps tapping down the stairs.

Darcy sagged down on the edge of her bed. She stared dismally at the other bed. It was freshly made up, a blanket folded at the foot. But gone were the colorful patchwork quilt Clemmie's mother had made, the Indian doll Clemmie had bought from one of the native women who sold their crafts by the railroad station. The bureau was cleared of all Clemmie's personal things. The room looked as empty as Darcy's heart felt.

SEVENTEEN

After Clemmie left, Darcy felt an intense loneliness. She felt lost without her friend. Tears came but didn't stop the ache in her heart.

If anything good could come out of this situation, it was that Clemmie's departure made the decision to accept Mrs. Ediston's offer easier for Darcy.

She knew she would miss Clemmie so much that it would be hard to welcome another girl as a roommate. Being a companion to the senator's wife would bridge the gap until maybe somehow, someday, the rift between the two friends could be mended. How that could be brought about, Darcy had no idea. She asked for a leave of absence and was given permission. Mrs. Ediston was delighted.

As Darcy packed her things to move out of the dormitory and into the hotel room adjoining Mrs. Ediston's, she came across the engagement ring she had never sent back to Grady. Quickly she gathered it with the half-written letter to her family, which she'd begun after Clara Bingham's insinuating question. She had to admit that keeping her real occupation from them had been wrong. She must finish the letter, not put this off any longer. Keeping secrets had got her in enough trouble.

Life as Mrs. Ediston's companion was much different from her strict routine as a Harvey Girl and took some getting used to for Darcy. To conserve her strength, Mrs. Ediston rose late, breakfasted at ten, and rested in the afternoon. This left Darcy with plenty of free time.

An unexpected bonus to this transition in her life was the developing relationship with Ted Shepherd. Ted had stayed on to supervise the early construction process of the Ediston's house. Now that Darcy had taken a leave of absence, the restriction on socializing with hotel guests was lifted.

Freed to be on equal terms, the two found each other's company enjoyable. Mrs. Ediston retired early, and Darcy and Ted spent many evenings together. Ted showed Darcy his renderings for the Ediston's new home, along with the blueprints, which he explained in detail. The house he had designed was beautiful. He had specified building materials suitable for the territory, in keeping with the landscape and the history of the land. Terra-cotta adobe walls, archways, timbered ceilings, tile walks, and locally wrought artistic ironwork balconies and railings were all integrated into the design.

Darcy was impressed by Ted's skill, his sensitivity to the environment, and his commitment to the integrity of his profession.

Besides the evenings they spent together, they also took several long-postponed horseback rides into the desert.

On these rides, Darcy got to know Ted Shepherd on a deeper level than she had the young men she had known, danced with, and flirted with back in Willowdale. This was true even from the first day.

As they rode out of town and onto one of the meandering roads that stretched into the desert, Darcy was aware that spring had come in profusion. Along each side of the road, which followed an old Indian trail, spread golden poppies, blue lupine, and pink clover in glorious color.

The blue sky seemed to go on forever. Spreading above them drifted fleecy formations of clouds evolving and dissolving. The sun turned the craggy rocks and canyons into a brilliant rusty red, and the air was as sweet and clear as a crystalline creek.

Everywhere they looked was a spectacular scene of nature's awesome splendor: Joshua trees, *Yucca brevifolia,* the tree lily of the Mojave Desert; giant saguaros outlined by the morning sun against the gold-washed jagged peaks.

As they rode, Ted surprised Darcy by initiating conversation, banishing her first impression of him as a quiet, introvert. He seemed eager to tell her about himself.

He was from a family he obviously cared about, including an older sister and a younger brother. His father was an engineer, his mother an artist.

"It's from her, I believe, that I get my draftsmanship skills. I can remember when I was just a little boy and she would take me with her out into the countryside, set up her easel to paint. She admired the French impressionists. And liked to paint *en plein,* outdoors in natural light. She wanted to paint visual images, not so much realistic renderings. So I guess I'm actually a combination of both my parents. Architecture has to be dimensionally correct, requires exact measurements and so on, but also you have to have an artist's ability to visualize the finished product, the right building in the right setting."

It was revealing to find out about Ted's background. The renderings he had made of the Ediston's house were artistic, almost paintings. Now she knew why.

They rode on in silence a little way until Ted began to speak again. "I know why Arizona is called 'the land of enchantment.'" He made a sweeping movement with one arm. "Look at this—have you ever seen anything so spectacular?" Darcy followed Ted's gesture. Was she seeing it all as he was seeing it? Spread out before them like a mural, the rusty red sand, the tortuously twisting rocks, the rugged canyons. The depths of the sky, the quiet of the desert. The strength of the majestic hills, monuments that had withstood centuries of sun, sand, wind, rain, and time—time beyond man's dreaming.

"Arizona is magical, mystical, mysterious, magnificent. There just aren't words to describe Arizona." Ted paused. "I can see why the Edistons want to live here. I hadn't a clue when they first commissioned me to come out here and find a building site for them. But"—he shrugged and smiled—"I was hopelessly smitten. I went back to Washington and revised my original plans for their house. Now it will fit in with the country. Adobe brick, balconies, cloisters. It will belong, not be some alien structure in this dramatic setting."

He glanced over at Darcy. "I guess you can tell I've come to love Arizona." He hesitated, as though considering whether he should say more. Then, as if satisfied with whatever he had been turning over in his mind, he said, "I've decided to resign from the firm I've been with in Washington. I have a few projects back there to finish, but the rest I'll turn over to some of the other architects. I want to come back here to live. I want to design and build my own house. Everything in complete harmony with the environment."

Darcy realized Ted was putting into words what she too had felt when she first came to Arizona. She had sometimes been almost overwhelmed by the beautiful desert country. It occurred to her that they had something deeply in common. Like herself, Ted had been touched, changed, by coming to Arizona.

It was almost noon when Ted pointed ahead. "There's a stream not too far from here. I thought it would be a nice place to rest the horses, let them drink." Soon they stopped, dismounted, and found a sheltered spot next to the serpentine creek, which was shadowed by the jutting rocks and surrounded by shrubby desert plants, misshapen cacti.

Ted took two canteens from his saddlebag and filled them with the sparkling-clear water, handed one to Darcy.

She drank thirstily, then glanced around. "This is incredible. It's so quiet. It's as though no one has ever been here before. As if we were the only two people on earth." She stopped, feeling a little shy about expressing herself so openly.

But Ted was nodding. "As my grandmother used to say—"

"You have a quotable grandmother? So do I."

"Yes," he said, smiling. "And I quote: 'Everything in nature is like a love letter from God.'" He paused, then added, "I really believe that although we cannot see God, he tells us about himself through his creation." He paused again. "The book of Genesis says, 'And God saw everything he had made, and behold it was very good.'"

Darcy was stirred. Something deep within her responded to what Ted was saying. She looked into Ted's eyes, which seemed so clear, so without pretense. This was a man of honesty and faith who was not afraid to express it.

Afternoon shadows lengthened, and in reluctant, silent accord they remounted and turned the horses back toward town. When they reached the hotel, Darcy said, "This was a wonderful day. I hate to see it end."

Ted looked at her thoughtfully. "There'll be other days like this, Darcy. I hope we can spend them together."

"I hope so, too, Ted."

There *were* other days together, other horseback rides into the desert country, before Ted left to go back to Washington. Darcy wondered if their companionship had any future. Maybe Ted had someone back east for whom he planned to build his house so he could bring her back to Arizona as his bride.

With both the senator and Ted gone, Mrs. Ediston and Darcy became very close. Of course, it was not the same kind of closeness Darcy had had with Clemmie. It was more like an ideal mother-daughter or aunt-niece relationship. She had begun collecting native pottery and was buying rugs and other artifacts made by the Hopi and Navajos. She also owned some original paintings by the famous western artist Frederic Remington and was having them shipped to Arizona for her new home.

"They belong here. Remington loved the Southwest with a passion, and you can see that in his paintings. They hung in my Washington home as a kind of dream wish. I prayed so hard for it, I can hardly believe I'm going to get my heart's desire. Which shows how little faith most of us have that God is willing to give us just that—as it says in Psalm 37."

Darcy discovered that Elizabeth Ediston was not only a cultured woman of great style but a deeply spiritual one as well. Mrs. Ediston's faith—she prayed about everything— made an impact on Darcy. She longed to have the same kind of faith. But first she had to clear up her guilty conscience. At long last she finished the letter to her mother and aunts, telling them the truth.

> *Dear Family,*
> *Before I tell you what I have kept from you because I thought*
> *you might not approve, I want to assure you I am well, better*

*than I have ever been in my life, and happier. At the moment
I am temporarily a companion to Elizabeth Ediston, Senator
Roger Ediston's wife, whom I came to know when they were
guests at the Harvey House hotel here. The reason I was able
to meet them was because I was working in the restaurant dining room as a Harvey Girl.*

Here Darcy paused. Was it possible that any of them
had heard about or read Clara Bingham's article about the
Harvey Girls? Had they possibly guessed that the waitress
she was writing about was Darcy? No matter. Darcy knew
she had to tell her own story, the whole truth. She began to
write again. Starting at the beginning, she described meeting Bertie on the train and her impulsive decision to apply
for a job as a Harvey Girl. She hadn't written the word *waitress*.

With a little shudder, she could just imagine what
combined gasps of disbelief would follow that.

Tapping her pen against the surface of the desk, Darcy
thought of the night she had given her life to God, confessed her sins, and made a commitment to turn over a new
leaf. It had been harder to do than she could have imagined
in that exalted moment. But the promise was that she could
become a new creature. "You need Jesus," the tract she had
nearly thrown away declared. She had read it over and over,
mentally blessing the anonymous person who had left it
there for her to find. Divine coincidence? She had recalled
the Scripture "Ye shall know the truth, and the truth shall
make you free," and had reworded the verse to fit her own
resolve: "Ye shall *tell* the truth, and the truth shall make you

free." She wanted to be free of the old yoke of telling the easy lie, making excuses, embroidering the facts. No, the only way was to put it all down on paper as it happened.

Finally she sealed and stamped the envelope. Darcy felt an enormous relief. But before she could mail the letter, she was caught in her own web of deceit.

EIGHTEEN

arvey House was all abuzz. The word spread like
wildfire. At first it was a rumor. Then as it traveled
the grapevine from national headquarters to the
managers' offices to the supervisors, the chefs, the head
waitresses, and eventually to the serving staff, it gained
momentum and finally force of fact.

It wasn't until Miss Cannon called Darcy to her office
that the whispers she had overheard were confirmed.

Although usually the epitome of composure, the head
waitress this day seemed tense. Bright spots of color burned
in her cheeks, and her blue eyes sparkled with excitement.
Once Darcy was seated opposite her desk, she said, "Harvey
House is going to have an unusual honor. The Rough
Riders are planning to hold their reunion here. I'm sure
you've heard of them?"

Of course everyone had heard about the Rough Riders, the voluntary group of men who had distinguished themselves in the famous battle of San Juan Hill during America's war with Spain. The returning soldiers had been welcomed as heroes, and many of them had become prominent in their local communities and in politics.

"There will be governors and mayors and state and county officials, along with their entourages, among those attending the reunion," Miss Cannon said. Then her eyes opened wider, and she added, "There is even a rumor that President Teddy Roosevelt, who was their leader, might be the keynote speaker at the banquet."

She paused for a minute. Then, seeming satisfied that Darcy was duly impressed by this information, she continued. "Whether or not the president attends, there will be an unprecedented number of important people coming. It is going to be a momentous occasion. Headquarters has ordered that the red carpet be rolled out."

Darcy was still not sure what all this had to do with her or why Miss Cannon had made a point of telling her about it.

"Everything is being planned to make it a grand affair in every way. The chef is creating a special menu. Of course, there will be need for extra service people."

Miss Cannon looked at Darcy with particular directness. "I know you are officially on leave of absence, but we want only our most experienced girls serving this banquet. There cannot be a misstep or an error of any sort. Service has to be as smooth as glass, everything perfect. There will be reporters and photographers here recording every detail of this occasion for newspapers all over the country. Harvey House's reputation will be at stake. This reunion must go off without a single flaw. That's why we are depending on our best waitresses to carry this off in fine style."

At last Darcy knew why Miss Cannon had called her in. *She* was to be among the specially chosen waitresses for this important banquet.

There were to be rehearsals even, as in a Broadway production. Everything had to proceed like clockwork, each course served with exact timing. The service had to be so seamless that it would not be noticed. The menu was printed and passed around to be memorized by the serving staff. The chefs practiced making the special dishes over and over so the final result would be a masterpiece of culinary art.

Darcy received her copy of the menu and studied it carefully.

Chilled Melon Halves
Tomato Bisque
Filet Mignon with Mushroom Sauce
Broccoli Hollandaise, Garden Peas, Mashed Potatoes
Head Lettuce Salad
Fresh Strawberry Mousse

Mrs. Ediston had been pleased to release Darcy for the days of preparation before the event. She was excited that Darcy would be part of the once-in-a-lifetime experience.

"The president is a very likable fellow, and his wife is charming," she told Darcy. As a senator's wife, Mrs. Ediston had attended many receptions at the White House and had met them both. "This is a day you'll remember all the rest of your life."

Darcy did not know how true that would turn out to be.

On the day of the banquet, the Harvey House staff was ready an hour before the arrival of the special train, to which extra cars had been added for the conference attendees. Crowds of local people were waiting at the station and began waving American flags when the train pulled into sight.

Darcy reported to the uniform room to pick up her official Harvey Girl outfit. After over a month of dressing so casually in shirtwaist and riding skirt and often in rugged boots, she felt a little strange in the uniform. A check in the mirror, however, transformed her back to the days when the starched bib apron over the black dress with its crisp, high white collar was her everyday attire.

Harvey House was using its very best waitresses, and she had proved herself to be one of those.

Her elation was deflated the minute she reported to the dining room for the pre-dinner rehearsal. In the line of neatly uniformed Harvey Girls was Clemmie! Darcy's first thought at seeing her was to immediately run over and hug her. But this impulse was nipped in the bud when her former roommate lifted her chin and pointedly turned her head at Darcy's approach.

Crushed, Darcy stepped into the line and tried to pay attention as Miss Cannon went through the precise order of service.

The tables in the dining room had been arranged together into a U shape so that everyone had a good view of the head of the table, where the most important dignitaries would be seated. Miss Cannon quickly squelched any speculation about whether the president would be there.

"Harvey House guests are all treated equally, with the same courtesy and careful attention to their needs. Water glasses are never left empty, nor coffee cups unfilled. Each course is removed only when the customer has put down his utensil, not before. Diners should not feel rushed, nor should they have to stare at a plate with uneaten food remaining upon it."

On and on her voice went, repeating all the rules that had been drilled into Darcy during her training. Her gaze kept returning to Clemmie, whose face was set, without even a flicker of friendliness. Darcy felt again the hurt of a lost friendship. She deeply regretted those few careless words she had spoken, words that had caused the unbridgeable chasm between them. This momentous event, which ordinarily would have been a shared occasion to discuss endlessly, now lay on Darcy's heart like a dead weight.

She didn't have time to think of her own feelings very long. Through the French doors opening from the dining room onto the courtyard, where the old war comrades were gathered, came the sound of laughter and male voices. The reunion had begun in full swing.

"Now, ladies, take your stations. Remember, Harvey House expects each one of you to make us proud," Miss Cannon said in a hushed but firm voice.

With a final hopeful glance in Clemmie's direction, Darcy moved to her station, which faced the doors leading from the courtyard into the dining room.

Even though for security reasons the guest list had not been disclosed, there was still a strong feeling among the staff that the flamboyant president might be among the attendees. There were rampant stories of how he often eluded his Secret Service guards to take unscheduled trips out of the White House or to play with his five rambunctious children on the lawns and tennis court. He just may have decided to join his former comrades-in-arms at this reunion. With this possibility in mind, Darcy searched the faces of the men flowing into the banquet room.

Then her blood turned to ice. Among the jovial groups still talking and laughing as they took their places, she recognized Dwight Michaels, one of Willowdale's county commissioners, a man well known to her Uncle Henry and a frequent visitor to the Beehive. That alone would have been bad enough, but worse still, in the group accompanying Michaels she saw Grady!

NINETEEN

D arcy's mouth went dry, her breath shallow. All the symptoms of panic. What was Grady doing here? Then she recalled that Michaels had served in the volunteer cavalry unit led by Roosevelt. It had been in Michaels' campaign flyers. However, she remembered hearing that Michaels had not come home a wounded hero but was discharged after contracting malaria.

All this raced through Darcy's mind while the dining room hummed with the noise of people conversing and finding their seats, giving her time to gather her wits.

And none too soon. As she drew a long breath to steady herself, Grady saw her. Something like an electric current went through her as he did. He went chalk white, then red. His eyes widened in disbelief. His mouth, under a newly acquired mustache, fell open.

He stood as if turned to stone, his gaze riveted on her. He stared at her, then made a jerky movement as if to come toward her. At that moment a man behind him touched his arm to speak to him, and Grady turned his head to answer.

At least Darcy had not been assigned to serve that side of the table. She wiped suddenly-sweaty palms on her apron and drew another long, shaky breath. Of all people, Grady was the very last person she had expected to see here, of all places. But then, Carly had mentioned in one of her letters that Michaels was considering running for governor of the state, and if Michaels had come, it would be natural for Grady to come with him. Michaels had been one of the men urging Grady to run for sheriff.

Now what? Guiltily she thought of the engagement ring still in the pocket of her valise, and the letter she had never written to him. There was no one to blame for this nightmare situation but herself.

The almost inaudible snap of the head waitress' fingers brought Darcy to attention. That was the signal to start serving the first course. She had to pull herself together, do her job. When the banquet was over, she would face whatever she had to face.

Automatically Darcy moved to the service counter, where the chilled melon slices were slid through the kitchen window for the waitresses to pick up.

Between the courses, Darcy sent furtive glances across the table, studying her former fiancé. In spite of the severe shock he must have suffered upon seeing her, Grady looked very well indeed. His appearance had changed significantly in the few months since she had seen him. Besides the mustache, which added some maturity to his boyish face, he was nattily dressed. Quite the dandy in a well-tailored sand gray suit, immaculate white ruffled shirt. All the rough edges of the country boy she had grown up with had been smoothed and polished. Whoever had been guiding his political ambitions had wrought a new image, no doubt carefully designed to make him more electable.

Darcy never knew how she got through the next hour and a half. Her movements were mechanical. She served course after course with trained precision, showing no indication that her emotions were in turmoil. When would Grady confront her? What was he going to do or say? Although he was sitting across from her section of the banquet table, she could feel his eyes continually upon her.

Her training was so ingrained that outwardly she was the perfect waitress, the ultimate Harvey Girl. As the dinner progressed and during the speeches that came afterward, Darcy wondered how long she could hold on. She felt like a condemned criminal with the noose tightening around her neck. There would be no reprieve from this sentence. An accounting was unavoidable. She would have no defense against Grady's furious interrogation.

Finally the dessert and coffee were served. Afterward the men, replete with good food and drink, began leaving the banquet table, drifting out into the inviting coolness of the courtyard under a star-studded Arizona sky. There the conviviality would continue, with more war stories, promises to keep in touch, plans for another reunion. It would be at least another hour before they would all return to the station and board the special train that would take them back to their respective towns and cities.

The busboys scrambled like ants as they cleared up, gathering the linen cloths, loading the trays with dishes and glasses, pushing the tables back into their regular formation. The weary waitresses, after receiving congratulations from Miss Cannon, were straggling out of the dining room, seeking well-earned rest.

Darcy looked for Clemmie. The shock of seeing Grady had temporarily thrust their still-unresolved breach out of her mind. Everything seemed to be crashing down upon her. Not that she didn't deserve it. Still, it left her feeling demolished and desolate.

"Darcy." The familiar voice struck the moment of doom into her heart. The dreaded moment had finally come. Straightening her shoulders, she slowly turned around to face Grady.

He was standing at the open French doors, hands clenched into fists at his sides.

"Well, Darcy, do you want to explain? If you *have* an explanation." The way he spoke, it sounded as if no explanation would be acceptable. His glance lingered on her uniform. He shook his head, bewilderment, anger in his expression. "Want to tell me what all this is about? What're you doing waiting on tables in that getup?"

Before she had a chance to answer, he demanded, "Does your mama know about this? The judge? What kind of a fool game have you been playing out here, Darcy? It just don't make any sense." He looked at her accusingly. "Your family don't know anything about what you're actually doing, do they? No, I didn't think so. I went by to see them before I left on this trip with Mr. Michaels, and your mother told me you had a new teaching job here in Arizona. Your Aunt Sadie showed me the postcards you sent her, telling her all about the Indian children and the pottery and the rugs and all that. Now I know it was all made up." His mouth twisted. "How could you do that to that poor old lady? To say nothing of your uncle and aunt—" He stopped. "How did you think you could get away with it? This don't seem to be any kind of joke. What's goin' on, I'd shure like to know?"

"I can explain, Grady, if you'd give me a chance." But then Darcy stopped. There really wasn't an explanation. She'd done a stupid thing and now she was paying for it. "I was going to write and explain, but—"

"Simply never got around to it? That just don't make sense, Darcy. Somethin' as important as being engaged, don't that deserve more than—" Grady shook his head again, as if this deception were beyond understanding.

"I'm sorry—," Darcy began, knowing it wasn't enough.

But Grady was too angry to listen. His indignation was building up. "I told everyone my fiancée was a teacher in this town! Dwight Michaels himself, possibly the next governor of Missouri, even suggested that I ask her to join us for dinner—as a *guest,* not a waitress!"

Frustrated even though she knew he had a right to be angry, Darcy interrupted. "Correction, Grady. Your *former* fiancée! Remember, I broke our engagement before I left Willowdale. You had no business telling him or anybody else that I was your fiancée."

"And I never accepted that either. I thought 'fore long you'd change your mind about marrying me. Everybody told me once you'd see what it was like out in the West on your own, you'd find out there's a lot of things worse than being a sheriff's wife."

"Which exactly proves my point. You never believed I meant what I said, that I didn't want to be a politician's wife. It didn't matter what I wanted. You thought you could bully me into being what you wanted me to be!"

Grady's expression changed. The belligerent look faded into one of doubt.

Darcy rushed on. "And I can see nothing's changed. You want me to be something I'm not. It still doesn't matter what I think or feel or want out of life."

Grady bit his lower lip, pausing as if to collect his thoughts before speaking. When he did, his voice was low and husky.

"I've loved you for a long time, Darcy, for as long as I can 'member. Since we were kids, actually. Why did you do this to me, make me look a fool?"

"Make you look a fool? I couldn't do that, Grady. If you feel a fool, that's your own fault. I think you're embarrassed to introduce me to your high and mighty friend, the possible governor. You're not seeing me; you're seeing this uniform. And you're ashamed to have them know what I do. That's what this comes down to. You don't love me for who I really am, what I am. It was fine when you could introduce me as a teacher. That was acceptable. Now that you find out I'm a waitress, you're ashamed of me, aren't you?"

Grady flushed. "It's you who oughta be ashamed, Darcy! You're the one who was ashamed to tell me and your family what you were doing. Shure, I was surprised to find out what you were really doing here in Arizona. But what I'm really shocked about is to find out you've lied."

That hit Darcy where it hurt. The truth always did. But she wanted the whole truth to come out now. "You're right, I did lie—and I *am* ashamed of lying! But I'm not ashamed of being a Harvey Girl! It's great. Harvey Girls are special and respected throughout the Southwest. Along the Sante Fe people say they are the best thing that ever happened to the West. And let me tell you this: I'm very good at what I do. Much better than I would have been as a teacher. And if you weren't such a snob, Grady, you'd understand that there's nothing shameful about it. It's a million times better than being a toady to some cigar-smoking politician!"

With visible effort Grady controlled his temper. "That's not what I am. It shure isn't what I intend to be, either. But I do want to be a sheriff, and for reasons that seem right to me, whether you agree or not."

Strangely, her indignation and anger began to simmer down. Darcy studied the man she had known all her life, the man she had considered marrying. Maybe she didn't understand him, his needs, his goals, his ambitions, any more than he understood her.

"Well, Grady, I think it's a good thing we found out all this about each other before we made the terrible mistake of getting married. I admit I was wrong to lie. And I'm sorry I hurt you. But maybe we're both better off in the long run."

Grady looked sad. "I don't know what's come over you, Darcy. I don't know you anymore. You're certainly not the girl I loved and wanted to marry."

Suddenly Darcy felt weary. There seemed no use trying to explain further. They had been apart too long. She had changed too much.

Almost wistfully she said, "Well, you don't have to marry me! You don't even have to tell anyone you *know* me."

Grady flung out his hands in a helpless gesture. "What am I going to say to your folks?"

"There's nothing for you to explain," Darcy said firmly, remembering Clara Bingham's words. "It's my problem and I'm going to take care of it."

An awkward silence fell. Grady started to ask, "Can't we—," then halted. Both of them knew it was too late. Even though they'd grown up together, they'd grown apart. Too far apart to find their way back to each other.

"I'm sorry, Grady," Darcy said and walked away without looking back, leaving him standing there looking after her.

TWENTY

Darcy started toward the dormitory steps, then stopped. She didn't belong there anymore. She had only been hired for this banquet, had only become a Harvey Girl again for this one special event. Like Cinderella when the clock struck midnight, after the ball she had nowhere to go. Instead she turned and walked out to the now deserted courtyard between the restaurant and the hotel.

She hugged her arms and walked slowly around the edge of the patio. As she walked, she could hear the soothing splash of the water in the circular fountain.

It was quiet, not a whisper of wind. The dark-blue sky was filled with stars. She sat on the brick edging of the fountain. From somewhere in the distance she heard the plink of guitar music. It was a familiar melody. A serenade, possibly. A romantic song she could not name, just feel in her heart, evoking a sweet melancholy.

She had lost Clemmie, her best friend, and Grady, her old beau, her childhood sweetheart, and once the truth of her deception was known, probably the respect and trust of her family and most of the people she knew in Willowdale. As if on cue, one of her Grandma Bee's sayings taunted, "Oh, what a tangled web we weave when first we practice to deceive." If she only had it to do over. . . .

Lost in her own thoughts, she did not see the tall figure who stepped out of the shadows, approaching slowly. Thinking she was alone, she was startled to hear her name spoken. "Miss Welburne? Darcy?"

She turned to see that it was Ted Shepherd.

"Ted! I didn't know you'd come back."

"I finished my work in Washington and took the first train back here I could get. I came in on the evening train. There was some delay along the way, a special train coming through or something. When I got here, I asked about you at the desk, and they told me you had worked a special banquet tonight."

She gave a short laugh. "Yes, indeed, I did work a special banquet."

"Is there something wrong? You seem—I don't know—sad somehow. Or am I being intrusive?"

"No, not at all." How sensitive he was to detect the irony in her voice. "I'm—well, not sad exactly, but. . ." She smiled ruefully. "It's just that I'm hearing the sound of the doors of my past banging shut one after the other, and I'm not sure if—" She paused. "Oh, I'm sorry. You don't want to hear all this."

"You're wrong. I do. I want to hear whatever it is that's making you unhappy."

"Closed doors are not reason enough?"

"It depends on what they've closed on. My grandmother used to say, 'When one door closes, another one opens.'"

Darcy was amused. "Your grandmother again?"

Ted laughed. "I guess all grandmothers are quotable. Maybe they all keep the same book of sayings, bring them out whenever it's appropriate." Ted came closer and sat down beside her. "Is there anything I can do to help?"

Darcy hesitated. If the veil of her deception was being ripped away, leaving her branded a liar, she might as well add Ted Shepherd to her list of lost friends.

"They say confession is good for the soul. So if you can stand it, I'll tell you. I'm warning you, though, it may change your wanting us to be friends."

"Nothing you could tell me would do that."

"Wait till you hear. I'm very ashamed of what I did, but it's all out in the open now, and I can't believe that I once felt the way I did."

Darcy began, "I come from a small town where values are pretty narrow. You are born into a certain place in society, and you're expected to stay there. I did come out west to take a teaching post, and..." Darcy told him about meeting Bertie and how she had decided to apply for a job with the

Harvey system. "I really liked it right away, but knowing how my folks back home would feel about it, I made the mistake of not telling them. It was silly, stupid, and I know better now, but I was too much of a coward then."

She sighed. "I just kept putting it off, and then—the proverbial ax fell." Darcy told Ted about talking to Clara Bingham and the article appearing in the *Ladies' Home Gazette*.

"Actually, it was a very positive story about how well-thought-of Harvey Girls are, but it exposed me as a snob and a liar." She looked at Ted to see his reaction.

He didn't look shocked, just interested and sympathetic. "We all make mistakes, do things we regret," he said. "But if we learn something valuable from them, I guess that's what counts."

"Oh, I've learned something, all right." Darcy sighed again, thinking of Clemmie's and Grady's reproachful expressions.

She stood up. "Well, confession may be good for the soul, but that's enough for one night. Thank you for being such a good listener." She took a few steps away, saying, "I'd better go."

"See you tomorrow?" There was a hopeful note in his voice.

"Oh yes, sure."

"Good night, then."

She had turned away to leave when his voice halted her.

"Darcy, remember—things usually look better in the morning."

She smiled in the darkness, a smile he could not see but which was in her voice when she responded, "Another of your grandmother's sayings?"

There was a soft chuckle. "Could be. I know I've heard it most of my life."

"So have I. I hope it's true. Well, good night again."

"Good night, Darcy."

TWENTY-ONE

nside the restaurant Darcy hesitated. It was late. She might disturb Mrs. Ediston if she returned to her adjoining hotel room. It wouldn't hurt if she slept in her old dormitory room for one night. Quietly she went up the steps. When she reached the upstairs hallway, she moved silently down the corridor to the room she had shared for so many months with Clemmie. For a moment she paused in front of the closed door before reaching out and turning the knob and opening it.

The minute she opened it, she stopped. She glanced around the room. To her total surprise the patchwork quilt and Indian doll were back on Clemmie's bed, and in the corner Clemmie was seated on a chair, unlacing her shoes.

Clemmie was back and acting as if their quarrel had never happened.

"Whoosh! What a night! My feet are killing me! How about you?" Clemmie asked casually.

Cautiously Darcy entered the room. Was Clemmie still angry, resentful? Had she finally forgiven her? "Clemmie, you're back! I'm so glad to see you," she said. "What are you doing here?"

"Called back. Emergency." Clemmie winked. "Only the best waitresses wanted for this shindig. That's me and you, I expect," she said with a cocky little shake of her head.

"Are you going to stay overnight?"

"I guess so. Truth is, I've missed being here." She hesitated, then said shyly, "Missed you too."

"And I missed you. Terribly."

Clemmie placed her shoes neatly together, then said, "Look, I'm sorry I took off in such a tiff. Once I got away, I realized you couldn't help what that woman, Clara Bingham, wrote." Clemmie paused. "If you want to know, my folks weren't all that happy about me coming out here to be a Harvey Girl. They put up a fuss, really, but I came anyway—" Clemmie paused again. "How could you tell such a whopper to your folks? And get away with it?"

Darcy sat down on her bed opposite Clemmie.

"Actually, I didn't get away with it." She sighed. "It's all come out now. Or will in a few days. Probably as soon as Grady gets back to Willowdale."

"You told him off but good." Clemmie blushed. "I overheard you. Didn't mean to eavesdrop, but I couldn't help but hear." She made a comic face. "You two weren't exactly whispering. You called in his cards, all right. I was bursting with pride when you told him how much folks around here think of the Harvey Girls. And to think we had our pictures taken with all the Rough Riders—a lot of them are mayors and county commissioners and stuff! And Teddy Roosevelt himself might have been there. If he had shown up, just imagine what our grandchildren would think of us having our photos taken alongside the president of the United States."

Darcy had to laugh. "Aren't you getting a little ahead of yourself? We aren't even married."

"Well, who's to say we won't be, and soon?" Clemmie put on a mysterious air.

"You've met someone," accused Darcy.

"You might say that." Clemmie preened. "A really nice fellow and a rancher. We've been going out and, well, it's pretty serious. I still have the rest of my year's contract to work. Then we'll make plans." She got all pink and her eyes danced. "What about you? That Ted Shepherd been back?"

It was Darcy's turn. She told Clemmie about Ted, how nice he was, her attraction to him. It was like old times, the two of them confiding in each other.

The next day, after Clemmie left on the train to return to her job at the Albuquerque Harvey House, Darcy knocked at the door of Mrs. Ediston's suite. In all honesty, Darcy felt she had to tell her employer everything, about how ashamed she was that she had lied and how sorry she was about everything that had happened as a result. It was an interview she shrank from, knowing Mrs. Ediston was the soul of integrity herself and expected high ideals of everyone. Darcy wasn't sure whether, when Mrs. Ediston knew the truth, she would still want her as a companion.

When she told her story, Mrs. Ediston listened attentively, then said, "All this just shows me how much you've grown since this"—she smiled—"charade began. Your values and your attitude toward work and others. I believe it's a worthwhile experience, no matter how painful it's been for you." Then Mrs. Ediston echoed what Ted had said. "We all make mistakes. Some are worse than others. You've only really hurt yourself. You may have misrepresented yourself to people to whom you should have told the truth.

"Now you can right that wrong," Mrs. Ediston paused. "Forgive yourself, Darcy. The Lord certainly has to forgive all of us a lot of things. I know from living in Washington all these years that people think what they want, believe what they want, make a great many false assumptions. Pride is the besetting sin among politicians. They want to look good to the public. If we hadn't come out here and I hadn't seen for myself what the Harvey Girls are like, I might have thought it was a menial job, too. You're afraid your family will be ashamed that you had taken such a job. But let me show you this." Mrs. Ediston reached for the pile of mail beside her chair and drew out a copy of the *Ladies' Home Gazette.* She held it up to Darcy. "I'm sure this looks familiar to you? It is one of the most popular and widely read periodicals back east. Maybe your mother and aunts subscribe to and read it as well?"

Darcy nodded.

"This is a letter to the editor from a newspaper columnist in Emporia, in response to Clara Bingham's article." Mrs. Ediston slipped on her reading glasses and read it aloud.

> *Dear Sir,*
>
> *I must add my accolades to the laudatory article published in your worthy journal about the Harvey Girls. From my personal experience and in my opinion, they are a welcome sight to tired travelers, a treat to their eyes, refreshment to their weary spirits, relief from their hunger and thirst when they alight from the train at any of the stations which are lucky enough to boast a Harvey House restaurant and hotel.*
>
> *Physically attractive in appearance, cheerful in disposition, poised in demeanor, gracious in service, courteous in manner, Harvey Girls in fact have all the qualities one could wish for in a friend, a companion, a spouse. The latter is perhaps the reason why there are always places to be filled in the Harvey system, as their elite ranks are constantly diminished by attrition to matrimony. But the standards for applicants are so high, it is my understanding that only one out of every ten who apply are selected for this exclusive group of young women.*
>
> *I would be proud to count any of my young female relatives among this highly sought after position.*

Mrs. Ediston finished reading, then glanced up at Darcy and smiled. "So you see, your young man should think twice before he rejects the idea of your change in profession."

"He's not my 'young man' anymore," Darcy said. "We've both changed too much. He was right when he accused me of not being the girl he'd fallen in love with— I'm not. I'm better, I hope. And I'm still trying to grow as a person. Something he couldn't possibly understand."

Mrs. Ediston closed the magazine and put it aside.

"Well, I'm both sorry and glad to hear that, Darcy. Sorry because it's always sad to outgrow someone we've cherished. But, it gives me the freedom to say that another young man is very much interested in getting to know you better." She paused. "Ted Shepherd. Roger and I have become very fond of him, and we admire him a lot."

Darcy felt her face warm. She felt it was too soon to say anything about her own feelings.

Darcy finally mailed her letter home. She felt as if a tremendous weight had been lifted. She'd had the confrontation she'd dreaded with Grady, made up with Clemmie, confessed to both Ted Shepherd and Elizabeth Ediston. Now she felt a glorious sense of freedom. Free to be her new self, free to live her new life, free to perhaps have a new love.

TWENTY-TWO

SEPTEMBER 1904

Their house nearing completion, the Edistons returned to Washington and to their official duties. They would return after the first of January, when the senator's term was over, and move to Arizona permanently.

Ted was staying on to oversee the finishing of the house's interior. Darcy returned to her job as a Harvey Girl.

The letters from Darcy's family came one by one. She dreaded opening them. She could almost have predicted the contents of each one.

From Aunt Maude, written in her bold, slanted script pressed so strongly into the stationery that she must have broken several pen nibs in writing it:

I am shocked, shocked beyond words, that a niece of mine would be capable of such duplicity. . . .

It went on in this vein for several pages, ending with a foreboding final paragraph.

I have not yet found the temerity to bring this information to your Uncle Henry. I shudder to think what he will say when he learns the full story of what you have done since you left home. . . .

From Auntie Sadie:

My Dear Little Girl,
Although you are hardly that anymore and must be treated as the woman you have surely become. To think that you acted with such courage in the face of such dire circumstances brings me to abject admiration. So far from home, with your plans totally shattered, you acted bravely to take the job offered to you. Even though it was the kind of position for which nothing before in your life had prepared you. I tried to explain this to your poor mama and Maude, but Maude felt sorry for Grady and couldn't think of much else. I have to hand it to him. He didn't say anything at all about you quarreling. Just that you looked very well and were happy in your work. He left it to your promise that you were going to write and explain everything. Which you did. Henry of course sided with Grady; men just don't like the idea of being jilted. Hurts their pride. Now don't you worry, dear girl. Your mama will come around, left alone without anyone (and I'm talking about sister Maude, for one!) fueling the flames. Again, you know how small towns are. As soon as this bone is passed around and chewed upon, something else will soon take its place. Remember, your old auntie is proud of you. I know it

took a lot of gumption to do what you did, and I don't blame
you one bit.

With love, Auntie Sadie

The last one she opened was from her mother.

Dear Daughter,
Everyone thinks I'm nursing a migraine brought on by your
letter. Nothing of the kind. But I did need some time to think
things through. First of all, I agree with you that Grady is
not the man for you, even though I don't agree with the way
you handled it. But who knows what is the best way? You
may be surprised that I thank God you two haven't gone
through with the wedding.

I look back and think I made a mistake in moving back
here after your father died. I let others influence my way of
thinking, and maybe let them take over some of my respon-
sibilities as your mother. Maude and Henry are fine people,
don't misunderstand me, but they look at things one way.
They regarded Grady as a good match for you and didn't
understand that you didn't want to live the same kind of life
in which you'd been brought up. So everyone has something
they're sorry about and need to be forgiven for.

I'm sorry you felt you had to lie to us. But I understand
why you did. We live in a tight little world back here in
Willowdale and probably care too much what other people
think and say about us.

Sadie gave me her copy of the Ladies' Home Gazette,
marking the complimentary letter from that journalist in
Kansas who wrote such high praise of the Harvey Girls.

I've never been a reader of the Gazette, *like Sadie has been all these years, following the romantic serials and all, but I looked over the whole issue this time and came to the conclusion that it is a fine periodical. So I'm ending this letter with something I saw printed in the personal section of the classified ads: "Come home, dear child, all is forgiven."*

Ever your loving Mother

Darcy read the letter through twice. She had never suspected that her mother was so understanding or had such a sense of humor.

"Come home, all is forgiven" indeed!

TWENTY- THREE

OCTOBER 1904

D arcy's one-year contract with the Harvey House system was over, and she made plans to go home. She had fences to mend, bridges to rebuild, hurt feelings to soothe, breaches of trust to heal, understanding and forgiveness to seek.

She was ready to do it now. A few months ago she wouldn't have been. She had a new source of strength, a new confidence, a new faith.

When she went to tell Miss Cannon good-bye, the head waitress said, "Well, I hope you'll be back and renew your contract. We don't like to lose one of our best Harvey Girls."

Darcy felt pleased. A year ago she might not have considered that a compliment. She had not even been sure she wanted the job. A lot had happened in a year, a lot had changed. Mostly Darcy had changed.

The day before she left for Willowdale, she and Ted took a horseback ride into the desert. It was late afternoon, and the sun's last golden gleams were a blend of pinks, blues, and purples.

The sculptured, arrow-shaped mountains rising into the sky were silhouetted against the red-gold glory of the sunset. They halted their horses to watch. A blaze of glorious color spread across the sky; then gradually the colors faded into twilight.

Night descended quickly in the desert after the drama of the sunset. As they rode back toward town, the sky darkened into a deep-blue canopy studded with stars. The night air was still and clear. The only sound was the whisper of wind.

Even though they deliberately slowed their horses, they soon arrived back at the hotel. The day was over. Their last ride together for who knew how long. Darcy felt an unnamed sadness. She did not know when she could return to Arizona. Or even if she would.

Ted got down from his horse, came around to help Darcy dismount. As she slipped out of her saddle, his hands went around her waist. For a minute they stood there, inches apart. Very aware of him, she drew back.

In a husky voice Ted asked, "What time does your train leave tomorrow?"

She told him, and then he said, "There might not be time tomorrow, or there might be other people around, so . . ." He reached into his jacket pocket and brought out a small, narrow box. "I'll give this to you now. Open it after you get on the train."

He leaned forward, lifted her chin in one hand, and kissed her lightly. It was a sweet, very tender kiss. When it ended, he started to say something else, then evidently changed his mind and just said, "Good-bye and God bless, Darcy."

As she walked slowly back into the hotel, Darcy wondered why Ted hadn't asked her if she was coming back. Everyone else had. Didn't he care? Or did he care too much to want an uncertain answer? But then, her own feelings were unsure. She had a growing excitement about going home. For the first time in this strange, eventful year, she admitted to herself how much she had missed her family, her friends, Willowdale. She was also curious about the outcome of the sheriff's election.

❧

The next day Arizona's fall weather was at its most beautiful—warm, sunny, blue sky, air like crystal. It all made it harder for Darcy to leave. She realized how much she had come to love Arizona.

Just as the train whistle blew its warning and Darcy was ready to board, Ted came running down the station platform. He reached her, out of breath.

"I had to see you off. I forgot to tell you something last night."

"What? What did you forget to tell me?" Darcy's heart suddenly raced.

"I forgot" — Ted swallowed — "forgot to say how much, how very much, I am going to miss you," he finished lamely.

Darcy was sure that wasn't what he'd forgotten to say. He seemed to be having second thoughts about what he wanted to tell her.

"All aboard, folks," the conductor announced and held out his hand to assist Darcy up into the coach.

All she had time to say was, "Thank you, Ted."

"Have a good trip!" Ted called. "And vaya con Dios!"

Darcy mounted the train steps, then hurried to find her seat so she could wave to Ted from the window. She pressed her face against the glass, looking back as the train moved down the track, gaining speed as it rounded the curve. Soon the adobe-brick station house and the tall figure on the platform waving his wide-brimmed hat were lost from sight.

After a few minutes Darcy remembered the little package Ted had given her and opened it. Inside was a beautifully crafted silver cross imbedded with turquoise stones, made by a Navajo artisan.

She clasped the chain around her neck, touching the pendant cross with caressing fingers. What a lovely gift Ted had chosen for her. She had come to cherish their friendship. She might have hoped for something more, something deeper. But maybe she wasn't ready for that yet.

As the train rattled across the prairie, carrying her back to Willowdale, Darcy thought back over the past year. Little had she dreamed, when she started her journey, how much she would change. She realized now that all the things she had thought were happenstance in her life were part of God's plan. The chance meeting with Bertie, becoming a Harvey Girl, her friendship with Clemmie, and the important night she had gone to church with her.

Two days later as the train pulled into the Willowdale station, Darcy peered out the window, scanning the platform, looking for the relatives who would be there to meet her. She spotted Auntie Sadie in one of her flowered hats; next to her was her mother, holding a bouquet of flowers; standing a little apart was Aunt Maude, looking stern but also excited. Even Uncle Henry was waiting there, looking dignified but, Darcy hoped, not judgmental. What he thought about her deception, she could only guess. He had not written as the other members of the Beehive had. Had he forgiven her for breaking her engagement to Grady and supposedly breaking his heart? He had certainly disapproved of her traipsing all over the country by herself and taking a job so far away. He was a gentleman of the old school. He firmly believed that a woman's place was in the home, under the roof of either her family or her husband.

Darcy sat on the edge of her seat, waiting for the train to come to a stop.

The minute she got off the train, she was immediately surrounded.

Her worries about Uncle Henry were unnecessary. He greeted her affectionately with the rest, and Darcy felt enveloped by her loving family. Of course, Carly was there, too. They hugged, laughing and crying at the same time.

A big party had been planned at the Beehive for her homecoming. A banner with "Welcome Home" in big letters was strung over the front door. Grandma Bee, in her best black silk and her lace cap, was waiting in the parlor. As Darcy bent down to kiss her cheek, the old lady commented tartly, "Come to your senses, have you, girl?"

In more ways than one, Darcy thought, smiling to herself, even though she wasn't sure she meant the same thing as her grandmother had.

The house was decorated with paper streamers, balloons, and flowers. Friends who had not been at the station were setting out platters of food, enough for an army, on the dining room table.

Darcy had always liked being the center of attention. She had forgotten how much she had missed that while being one of the uniformed Harvey Girls. It was fun and pleasant to stand with her mother and aunts and receive the warm greetings of old friends and acquaintances.

Then suddenly she saw a tall figure coming through the door. Grady! It wasn't until he was only a few feet away from her that she saw the silver star gleaming on his chest. The sheriff's badge! So Grady had won the election.

Now he stood right in front of her. He held out his hand and, speaking softly, with the old tenderness, spoke her name.

She hesitated a few seconds, then took his hand, smiling. "Sheriff Thomas. What an unexpected pleasure. I thought you'd never want to see or talk to me again."

His face reddened slightly. "Ah, Darcy, let's let bygones be bygones. I don't hold with keeping a grudge." He grinned. "I'm a peacekeeper. That's what it said in my pledge when I was sworn in. A sheriff's purpose is keeping the peace."

"Of course," Darcy said with some surprise. She sensed a seriousness in him, a maturity, a certain confidence. Perhaps in the year they had been separated, he too had grown and developed and changed.

However, there was still something of the old teasing twinkle in his eyes. They had shared too many good times together, too much laughter and fun, to forget, to not appreciate and remember.

"Well, Grady," Darcy said, pointing to his badge. "It looks as if you got what you wanted."

His smile faded. "Not all that I wanted. Maybe not the thing I wanted most."

She returned his searching look. "Nobody does, Grady. That's one thing I've learned this year."

"Guess you're right, Darcy."

Grady shifted from one foot to the other. He seemed to want to say more, to prolong this brief meeting. People in line behind him, waiting their turn to greet her, stirred restlessly; others were looking at them curiously.

"Will you be staying now?" he asked.

"I'll be here until after Thanksgiving—then I'm not sure."

Something curious flickered in his eyes, and he said shyly, "I sure—we all missed you." Then he moved on.

Later that evening in her old room, ready to go to bed, Darcy thought over the events of the day. The warm affection showered on her, the genuine pleasure everyone seemed to share at her being back in Willowdale. "Back where you belong," her uncle had said several times. Was this after all where she belonged?

She fingered the silver cross and chain Ted had given her. Looking at the beautifully crafted Indian design, she felt a nostalgia for all she had left in Arizona. She thought of the wide skies, the distant hills, the cactus flowers of the desert. Her heart was filled with longing.

But then, it was also wonderful to be home, to see familiar faces, to feel the love and hear the good wishes of people who had always known her. Tonight Arizona seemed a very long way away.

Seeing Grady today had been an emotional experience. Maybe she would have been perfectly happy if none of the events of the past year had ever happened. If she and Grady had married as they had planned, settled down here in the pleasant valley of Willowdale, raised a family—maybe it would have all worked out. She would never have known the possibility of any other kind of life.

But maybe that had never been meant to be. Maybe she was destined to go to Arizona, to see new horizons, to find a new life in a beautiful new land, to meet Ted Shepherd. Her heart was divided. Only time would tell. She would pray and think about it.

❧

JANUARY 1905

Darcy changed trains in St. Louis and settled contentedly into her coach seat. She was on her way back to Arizona. Clemmie was marrying her rancher and Darcy was to be her maid of honor. She had also written Miss Cannon to tell her she wanted to renew her contract as a Harvey Girl for another year. After that, who knew? Whatever happened, Darcy was convinced it would be God's plan, not hers. She no longer made impulsive decisions nor "leaned on her own understanding." There was a better way, a truer way—she had learned that at last.

Two days later when the train pulled into the station at Redsands, Darcy looked out the window. To her delighted surprise, Ted was standing on the platform. She had sent him a note that she was coming, but she had not counted on his meeting her. He must be very busy now that the house he had designed for himself was under construction. But she was thrilled to see him. In that first moment she was convinced that returning to Arizona was the right thing to do. She had followed the call of her heart to come back, and she had found her heart's true home.

The train came to a stop, and she stood up, gathered her belongings in preparation for getting off. Before she moved down the aisle to the door, she drew out from her handbag a thin booklet and lay it on the seat she was vacating. It was the tract with the bold statement "You need Jesus," which someone had left for her to find over a year ago, when she had first started her long journey. Now she was doing the same for someone else. She had learned the truth of it, and the truth had set her free.

If you like this book, check out these other great books by Jane Peart!

Brides of Montclair Series

Shadow Bride
Softcover 0-310-66951-0

Courageous Bride
Softcover 0-310-20210-8

A Montclair Homecoming
Softcover 0-310-67161-2

Westward Dreams Series

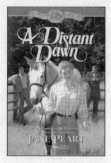

A Distant Dawn
Softcover 0-310-41301-X

Undaunted Spirit
Softcover 0-310-22012-2

Pick up a copy at your favorite bookstore today!

ZONDERVAN

GRAND RAPIDS, MICHIGAN 49530

www.zondervan.com

We want to hear from you. Please send your comments about this book to us in care of the address below. Thank you.

ZONDERVAN

GRAND RAPIDS, MICHIGAN 49530

www.zondervan.com